Solomon Revealed

J. W. Edwards

Solomon Revealed

Back to the Beginning
To Ignite the Future

L. W. Edwards

First Edition
First Printing 2017
L.W. Edwards
Solomon Revealed
Summary: Mystery novel featuring Addie Conroy,
private security professional.
ISBN: 978-9860562-2-2
Book format by Penury Press, LLC
Cover design by Penury Press, LLC
Author Photo by Jennifer M. Tjernagel - Studio 241 Photography
Black Onyx Press
Shakopee, MN
www.blackonyxpress.com
Printed in the United States of America

There are mysteries that have been revealed;
twenty-four in all,
Some of them lower, some of them higher,
Some of them will sear the soul.

CHAPTER 1

"Clocks, keys, secret maps and now a late Wolff," If he didn't show up soon, Jacob would leave him to fend for himself. Just then, Jacob heard the ever-so-soft sound of boots crunching on rock, coming from behind the jeep. The heat index in Panama was bad enough; add the adrenaline rush and it felt ten degrees hotter. He turned slightly in his seat and brought his gun up to the open window just as Mr. Thaddeus Wolff popped his head up.

"Man, you're getting old and slow," Jacob said. His gun was slightly touching the end of Wolff's nose. "I heard you as you went around the back of the jeep."

"No way, I saw you turn just seconds before I popped up to meet your poor excuse for a weapon. How many years ago did I tell you to get rid of that thing? I could hear it when you took the safety off," Wolff told him. He leaned into the gun until Jacob finally lowered it back onto his lap, this time he did so without putting the safety on.

"It's my lucky gun! If you weren't one of Addie's pets I would've just shot you," Jacob added.

"Yeah, and you want me to believe you spent three nights in a cave up in those hills?" Wolff said. He was leaning on the jeep window with his face a little too close to Jacob's. Wolff was looking for a clue as to whether or not Jacob was lying. At the very least, he wanted Jacob to admit where his hideout was. "Fess up cave man, you have a ladies' den somewhere, not a cave in the jungle."

"Nope, that's your gig man. No She-Wolff's around me, just a dirt floor in a cave that keeps me out of the rain. I can live anywhere above or below ground with or without anyone and still look great. If you want, I'll teach you," Jacob said, leaning back in the jeep's seat trying to appear bored. Wolff could see no sign of deception anywhere on his face.

1

"Show me? I'm a Wolf, not a mole," Wolff said. He walked around to the passenger side and opened the door.

"Get in, you dog. Good thing I chose the jeep, you're attracting flies, where to man?"

"You remember that little out-of-the-way airfield Solomon has inland from Anton Valley?" Wolff asked.

"Know it? I helped design it. I could find it in my sleep. But I refuse to drive that far with you smelling like this. We'll make a stop at a place I know."

Before he could continue, both their phones vibrated at the same time.

"Hey Snoop. Way ahead of you. We're together already, putting you on speaker now," Wolff told him.

"Great, before you head out, I need you two to hit the hospital and get the clock before you meet Addie at the airfield," Snoop instructed.

"Is that why I've been hunkered down under a pile of brush watching that old hospital?" Wolff asked.

"Yeah, and what of it? Goes with the job my man," Snoop answered. Wolff shook his head and looked over at Jacob, who had a smug smile on his face.

"Snoop, we don't need to go to the hospital to get the clock. I already have it," Jacob answered.

Wolff stared at Jacob and that smug look on his face. "What do you mean you have it? When did you take it?" Wolff asked.

"Yesterday," Jacob answered.

"You're lying; Snoops had me guarding that hole for the past three days. No way, you got past me."

"Oh? But I did, my man. So that means you're either getting old, your eyesight is going or I'm just better than you," Jacob answered.

"None of the above. Now, show me the clock," Wolff demanded.

"I ain't taking your dirty-dog-self anywhere until you're cleaned up," Jacob shot back.

"Boys, I don't care how you work it out and who got what, as long as you have that clock and get it to Addie. I do, however, want to know one thing. Jacob, what made you go back for the clock?" Snoop asked.

"Instinct," Jacob answered.

"Bull," Wolff spat back.

"Well boys, let me break it down for ease of understanding. Addie insisted I look for the key to the clock, then open the drawer and take out anything that's inside. I was also instructed to take pictures of the engraving on the sides of the clock's cabinet right Snoop?"

"Yeah," Snoop answered.

"Well, I did all that and took it back to the cave. For the next couple of days, while I was waiting for your call, I had a lot of time to look at the pictures. I must have looked at those pictures a thousand times before it hit me. The edges of the clocks cabinets looked like they were tongue and groove carved, at least from the pictures Addie sent of the clock from Cassie's house. I think if you stood them next to each other, the edges would fit together. The clock I have must be the middle one because there are grooves on both sides. That would mean Cassie's, and the other one, are end pieces. Depending on how they fit together, they could form a half circle. I just had to see if I was right, so yesterday I decided to go back and get the clock," Jacob told them.

"Where is it? Is it safe?" Snoop asked.

"Safe as safe can be," Jacob answered.

"And how would you know how this tongue and groove stuff fits together?" Wolff asked.

"I was the son of a carpenter and in his spare time he liked to try and duplicate the old ways. I've made almost all my own furniture," Jacob answered, smiling at Wolff. "Buckle up," said Jacob. The jeep lurched forward, throwing Wolff towards the dashboard.

"Tell her we're on our way," Wolff said, holding on tight to the side of the jeep.

3

"Do you know where you're going? And why do you always go places where there are no roads?" Wolff asked.

"Roads are watched and can be blocked. Girls take roads. Well, except for the girls who work for Addie. Don't worry Wolff, you'll survive," Jacob answered. As he hit the next bump, Wolff's head hit the roof of the jeep.

Wolff didn't say anything. He just leaned back in his seat, pulled his cap down over his eyes and tried to doze off between bumps.

"Hey sleeping beauty, we're here," Jacob said. As he slammed on the brakes, Wolff was propelled forward against his seat belt.

"And where is here? We're in the middle of nowhere," Wolff asked.

"You're getting so whiney in your old age," Jacob shot back.

"Jacob, we're the same age," Wolff reminded him.

"Yeah, but you act older than me. Come on, I know a man who has a place right through those trees," Jacob said. From behind him, he heard the rustling of branches. Wolff, always on guard, pulled his gun.

"Wolff, put it away, it's just kids," Jacob said, calling out their names as Wolff lowered his gun. Two small heads peeked out from behind the heavy foliage and ran to meet Jacob.

Wolff watched as Jacob pulled candy out from behind their ears and then pointed to the jeep. Wolff was amazed as the two boys went into action.

From behind one set of bushes, they pulled a camouflage net and started covering the jeep, adding some of the nearby foliage to complete the job. The jeep was fully covered in no time. Jacob pretended to inspect the job and then turned around, saluting the two kids as he handed each one a coin.

"Come on Wolff, let's get you cleaned up," Jacob called. As he parted the low branch, Wolff saw the entrance to a path that was cut through the deep vegetation.

"Jacob, don't tell me those are your kids. Who are these people?" Wolff asked, rushing to keep up with Jacob. There was no way he was getting left behind out here.

"Who knows if their mine or not, as for who they are, they're one of many small tribes scattered throughout this country. Who really knows who they are, that's what I like about it, there is so much left to explore. I spent about three months living out here, while on a job that Trask contracted for me. It was awesome."

"Are you serious? Out here in this God forsaken jungle...," Wolff was cut short when Jacob once again pushed aside branches, blocking the view of a large clearing that was dotted with huts on stilts. Standing close together in the bright sun was a line of beautiful people with skin that looked like bronze in the sunlight. Wolff followed Jacob, who was waving to them. The men smiled and waved back while the women waited for them to approach. The children started racing to meet them.

Wolff watched as Jacob gathered up one of the little boys and showed the others that he could pull candy from his ear. Once the kids saw the candy, Jacob was immediately mobbed. Patiently, the elders waited until each child had received his treat and Jacob moved toward them. Wolff followed at a distance behind Jacob. While Jacob had been handing out candy, Wolff was observing the tribe and it was obvious there was a distinct pecking order.

When they reached the head of the tribe, Wolff watched as Jacob conversed with him and waited for the chief to respond. Walking forward he embraced Jacob like a long-lost friend and pointed at Wolff. Jacob shook his head and whispered to the Chief, who looked over at Wolff as though he felt sorry for him.

"Jacob, what did you tell him?" Wolff asked, following behind him as the Chief led them to a hut.

"I just told him you needed refreshing," Jacob answered.

"You're a liar," Wolff hissed.

"Okay, so I told him you needed to get out of the sun and could he do anything about you smelling like a monkey."

"Why you...," Wolff stopped short when they entered the hut where two young women stood talking to the Chief. Once he'd finished speaking to the women, he seated the two men. What seem like only seconds later, the women returned with bowls of food balanced on their shoulders. They were served immediately and continued being served until they were stuffed.

"Man, what did I just eat? It was delicious," Wolff asked, smiling back at the beautiful young lady that was now handing him a cup of water.

"You seriously don't want to know. Let's just say it's definitely at the bottom of the food chain," Jacob answered. He watched Wolff swallow hard and then take another quick drink.

"Great and now I'm so full I need a nap,"

"No naps. We're going to get cleaned up and then go out the back way. We have a clock to deliver, remember?" Jacob answered standing. Wolff followed suite and stood up.

The next thing Wolff knew he had two young women on each side of him removing his clothes.

"Hey Jacob, what gives?" Wolff asked. He tried to gently push their hands away and re-button his shirt, before things became awkward. He looked over at Jacob, whose ladies were wrapping what looked like a bed sheet around his waist.

"Wolff, let them do their job. Don't worry, they won't hurt you. Man, when did you turn into such a prude?" Jacob asked.

6

"Prude? I'll show you who's a prude," Wolff answered. Kissing the lady's hands, he straightened his shoulders and held out his arms, following the ladies lead. An hour later, the ladies were finished with him and he felt like a new man. According to Jacob, he also smelled like a new man. Fatigue no longer an issue they were on their way trudging down another path that ended at a slightly better dirt road. Parked on the side of the road was a brand new black SUV, motor running, and being guarded by several boys.

"Wow, where did this come from?" Wolff asked.

"Solomon Inc., don't ask me what kind of deal they made with the chief and who does the dealing, probably Snoop. All I know is, whenever I need anything, all I have to do is come here and everything is supplied, no questions asked and no charge."

"Tell me something," Wolff asked.

"If I want to," Jacob said.

"You know, that attitude of yours sucks Jacob."

"Like yours."

"Point taken, my question is, do those women just?" Wolff said.

"Do you mean the ladies that bathed us?" Jacob asked.

"Yes, those ladies. You said you stayed there for three months. Did any of the ladies like you?"

"Lots of them, but most of them are married. The two that bathed me, I guess you could say they were assigned to me when I was living there. How can I say it, so your delicate ears can handle it, basically I didn't need blankets?" Jacob said.

"Are you serious, and then you just left them?" Wolff asked.

"Are you serious, it wasn't like I could take them with me, you know we can't travel like that. Remember your training, don't stop moving and never acquire anything you can't walk away from or leave in an instant," Jacob said. His

7

voice made Wolff feel like a kid that had just been scolded by his big brother.

"I remember, but I also remember family. Man, have you really gotten that cold?" Wolff asked.

"No, I've gotten that smart and that careful. You saw the way the two ladies handled me. I left them with good memories. If I hadn't, they would have given me to the other women or worse, they have poison darts you know. Wolff, if you have to leave them, leave them with good memories or don't leave them with any," Jacob told him as he hit the gas.

CHAPTER 2

"Man, slow down. Addie wants us there in one piece," Wolff said. He was holding on for dear life, thanking God he had a seatbelt and the SUV was a smoother ride.

"Wow, you're a prude and a baby. What's happened to you man? The faster the better, as I remember it. No one could keep up with you," Jacob said, hitting the gas again.

"Yeah, well it gets old Jacob. Don't you ever think about settling down like Addie has?" Wolff asked. He was starting to get into the rhythm of the SUV now. He braced himself in a position to ride with the bouncing, thinking that his old training was coming back, like it always did.

"Man, what are you talking about? Addie didn't settle down, all she did was get married."

"She married a civilian," Wolff said.

"Yeah, but she's not working for Uncle Sam anymore and she left on good terms Addie isn't running from anything, so she's free to tell Martin about her life, within reason. I'm sure she doesn't discuss sealed files or talk about the inner workings of Solomon. I mean, Martin's in danger, but not like us. I feel sorry for the families of some of the militaries finest, that have no idea how much danger they could be in," said Jacob.

"Especially given our current terrorist climate, everyone's at risk these days. Everywhere I've traveled in the last ten years, man you can just feel the love for old Uncle Sam," Wolff added.

"Yeah and all those innocent people, they never see it coming. Martin knows what his wife does and what the risks are, he's always on guard, taking precautions. I'm sure he either has been trained or will be. So, what's up with you Wolff, you got someone on the outside that you're serious about? I need to know that your head is here," Jacob said.

"My head is here; don't you worry Jacob. There isn't anyone, I'm just thinking about when I retire. Where are you taking us?" Wolff asked.

"To get some flowers," Jacob answered.

"Flowers? What the hell do we need flowers for?"

"To pay our respects," Jacob said.

"We don't' have time for sentimental journeys, we have to get that clock and...," Wolff started to say.

"There he is. That's the old Wolff I know. Believe me man, we have time for this," Jacob said, smiling over at Wolff. He sped up the road, but started to slow as they came to a small village. Both Jacob and Wolff searched the county side as the SUV slowly made its way to the center of town. Without getting out of the SUV, Jacob drove up to a small flower stand where a beautiful lady stepped forward with a bouquet of brightly colored flowers. She smiled at Jacob, who handed her a rolled-up bill. In return, she handed him the flowers and leaned forward, kissing him full on the mouth, while using the flowers to block the kiss from public view. She then stepped back and waved goodbye as Jacob drove off. Jacob hit the gas pedal hard and threw the flowers at Wolff.

"You got women everywhere?" Wolff asked, laying the flowers on his lap.

"Only where I need them," Jacob answered. He drove out of the city to the town's graveyard. Wolff observed it was within walking distance of the town, which was fitting for the ceremonies of the area. By tradition, they walked behind the wagon to the graveyard, but far enough out so that they were no longer in view of their deceased loved ones. The women of the town said that this ritual made it a little better for those in mourning. It was the middle of the week, and early in the afternoon, so the locals would still be working. If they were lucky, they would be alone in the graveyard.

Jacob didn't stop at the graveyard. Instead, he continued driving out of town. Jacob rounded a hill and pulled into a path that seemed to lead right into the jungle. Wolff held on tight to the handle near the SUV's window, and the flowers, as Jacob followed the rough path through the jungle until he came to a small clearing.

Jacob parked the SUV and looked over at Wolff, "Grab a kit, while I cover the SUV, there's one for each of us. Make sure you don't forget the ghillie suits, I know how you love dressing up," Jacob said, while he pulled a cover from the back seat and covered the SUV. Grabbing his gear he dressed and headed for the rock ledge, crawling on his knees. Wolff, finding his stride, was right behind him. Wolff could see a rock ledge up ahead and followed Jacob. He dropped to his knees and made his way to the end of the ledge beside him. Looking over, Wolff could see that they were above and behind the cemetery. There was one large crypt at the back, up on a small hill, which looked as if it was keeping watch over the rest of the small mounds and tiny markers.

"They were the founders of the village, back when that kind of thing mattered," Jacob told Wolff.

"And that matters to us how? If we weren't going to pay our respects, why did we buy flowers?"

"We will leave them for the lady of the house," said Jacob.

"Look at the back of the crypt," Jacob said.

Wolff pulled out his glasses. At first, he didn't see anything but the stone at the back of the crypt. But then, as he focused in on the wall, he noticed a small, very faint line. He could see an outline of what looked like a door, which was not covered with moss like the rest of the wall, was.

"So, I take it there's a back door?" Wolff asked Jacob.

"You take it right. Wolff, you look so good in that suit, if the ladies could see you they'd be all over you," Jacob said smiling. He rolled over, pulled out his blade and cut some long palm branches close to them as cover. Wolff followed his lead, and the two snipers settled to watch.

It didn't take them long to spot visitors. Wolff pulled his glasses up to his eyes and looked down at the small crypt. He watched a young woman dressed in a white sun dress and a wide brimmed soft yellow hat walk to the front of the building. Flowers in hand, she divided the bouquet and placed half of the flowers in one urn, and the other half in the second urn, that were set on each side of the steps leading up to the crypts door. She then stood there silently for a few minutes with her head bowed.

"She looks so familiar," Wolff said.

"She should and she's. trouble," Jacob answered. "She's one of us, but she is definitely not on our side."

"You were followed my friend. Who's slipping now? They know you were here and are waiting for you," said Wolff. He was feeling much better now that he could point out an imperfection of Jacob's.

"Maybe or maybe not," Jacob answered, scanning the area for signs of other snipers.

"What now?" Wolff asked.

"How about you go down and get the clock?" Jacob said smiling.

"Right, smart man you got any other bright ideas?"

"Yeah, I think I'll take out the guy on the right, over on that hill," Jacob said.

"And I'll take out the guy on the left over there. You can't have all the fun. By the way, do you think she's armed?" Wolff asked.

"Old friend, that woman is armed even when she is naked in bed. I would say she has no less than three weapons on her right now, but you know my rule," Jacob said.

"Yeah, I know no women and no children. You do what you have to, she's all yours," Wolff answered. Jacob took the first shot, and a second later Wolff took his. Both men looked over at their kill zones and knew instantly that they

12

made direct hits. Jacob took the third shot whispering under his breath. "Sorry baby, I'd rather put you to sleep a softer way, but you chose the wrong side," Wolff watched as the next shot just grazed the side of her head before she could take cover. She went down hard over the front steps of the crypt. They waited a couple few minutes letting the late afternoon shadows block off part of the crypt. When no more shots came, they were down the hill behind the crypt and inside.

Once inside, they spared no time opening the coffin to verify the clock was intact. While Jacob replaced the lid, Wolff looked through the window to the front to make sure their lady friend was still out-cold, but she was gone.

"Jacob, we need to watch our backs man! Your shot didn't keep her out," Wolff called back to him.

"It kept her out someone must have picked her up. Hey, I could use some help in here," Jacob said from deep inside the crypt.

Wolff joined him beside the coffin that was atop the obelisk, in the center of the room.

"You want the head or the tail?" Jacob asked smiling.

"I'll take the foot. Just a thought before we start, aren't we going to look a little suspicious carrying a coffin out of a crypt? I'm pretty sure that, even in Panama, there are laws against this sort of thing," said Wolff

"Only if we get caught and only if there's a body. There isn't a body and I don't plan on getting caught. I'm surprised you don't remember the first rule we learned in training."

"Which rule would you be referring to, old buddy?" Wolff asked.

"Never go back the same way you came. Now, help me pull this up," Jacob said, disappearing behind the coffin.

Wolff rounded the side of the coffin to see Jacob brushing the dust away from a spot on the floor of the crypt. He then grabbed an iron ring, but struggled to pull it upward. Wolff joined him and together they moved the heavy piece of stone that was used as a trap door. Moving the stone revealed a rugged set of stone steps. Jacob and Wolff didn't waste any time moving back to the coffin. They quickly lifted it upwards and Wolff followed Jacob's lead down the steps.

They didn't talk, they just kept moving without looking back. Jacob and Wolff found themselves walking down a short flight of steps into a dirt tunnel that had a ridiculously low ceiling, forcing both men to crouch down to keep from hitting their heads. The tunnel went on longer than Wolff anticipated. Jacob stopped and set his end down, motioning for Wolff to wait for his queue. Wolff set down his end and took a ready position, just in case, as he watched Jacob disappeared into the darkness ahead of him.

Wolff heard what sounded like a door open and then heard Jacob's voice talking to someone. Still on guard, gun ready until, Jacob reappeared and gestured for Wolff to put the gun away and pick up his end of the coffin. Wolff followed Jacob to the small door at the end of the tunnel, where a man was standing in the shadows. Their SUV was waiting just a few feet outside the door. They loaded the coffin and Jacob covered it with a tarp that was on the back of the SUV. Jacob then turned and slipped the old man some money. Wolff was already in the driver's seat.

"Hey man, you know the way to Trask's place?" Jacob asked, climbing in shotgun.

"I've been there once, but since I have you here, you can direct and I'll drive. I'm sure once we get close I'll remember the way," Wolff answered, gunning the engine and leaving the area in a cloud of his dust.

"I guarantee you won't remember the way," Jacob answered, buckling his seat belt and gripping the door frame.

"You think my memory's that bad?" Wolff asked.

"You already forgot. I never go...," Jacob started to say.

"I know, I know, the same way twice. OK then, which way?" Wolff asked, as they came to a fork in the road.

14

"Left," Jacob answered and smiled.

CHAPTER 3

"Addie, are you awake?" Addie heard Martin ask softly. He had rolled over and cuddled up behind her, pulling her close.

"I'm awake," Addie answered. She didn't know how she was going to explain to him that she was more afraid, than mad, to have him here.

"Are you speaking to me yet?" Martin asked, softly kissing her back.

Addie rolled over to face him. He was looking at her with that wounded little boy face.

"I'm always speaking to you Martin," she answered, leaning in for a kiss. "I just wish you and Nick were at home, safe and sound."

"I wish you were too every time you go out on a job. I just thought if I came along once, I would see how good you are and I wouldn't worry so much the next time. Besides, I think Nick and I are safer here than we were at home."

Addie smiled. "You may be right they did put bombs in the backyard."

Martin pulled her close again and kissed her. "You still love me?" He asked hopefully.

"I do my sweet husband. If I didn't, I would have shot you when I found you," She answered, kissing him again.

"Addie, I don't want you to worry about me. If something happens, this is where I chose to be, with my wife. I would rather die beside you then be blown up at home without you."

"No one is going to die on my watch. Besides, it's a good thing you came. I need all the prayer cover I can get, and my men can't give me that, but you can," Addie said, pulling away as she rolled out of bed.

"You mean you were serious about making me work? Come back to bed," He pleaded, patting the place she'd just left.

"You're going to work like you've never worked before you're on the job now. As for coming back to bed, we're on a job Martin. I have other operatives that can use this bed to rest, so we give it to the guys who have been up all night on assignment," she told him. She quickly pulled on her clothes and left the room.

Martin rolled on his back. Wow, this wasn't what he'd expected, but the more he thought about it the more he realized she was right. This was not a vacation. They were on a serious job and there was a team to think about, a team that Addie was responsible for. Martin sighed, said a prayer, and rolled out of bed, pulling his clothes on fast. He made a quick stop in the bathroom and then headed out to the main cabin.

"Hey man. Did you sleep well or did our Addie make you work all night?" Ray asked.

"No such luck, she reminded me that we're on a job," Martin answered.

"Sorry man, your woman is a professional. She takes her work very seriously, but at least when you both go home you have each other. Most of the rest of us aren't that lucky. Want some coffee?" Ray asked.

"I do and thanks for reminding me how lucky I am."

"Ray, Addie's looking for you. She's in the conference room," Bird said.

"Go ahead Ray, I'll get my own coffee, Addie needs you," Martin told him.

Ray smiled back. *Martin would be okay*, he thought as he turned to follow Bird.

Martin had just poured a cup of coffee and turned to go back towards the main cabin when he heard Nick's voice come over the airplane's paging system.

17

"Please be seated and fasten your seat belts. ETA is set for ten minutes from now and it could be a rough landing." Martin smiled to himself. Nick must be eating this up. He grabbed for a lid for his coffee, making sure it was tight, before leaving the kitchen. Martin walked into the main cabin and sat in a plush seat next to a small table that was placed in front of a window. The sun was bright as it lit up the surface of the fluffy white clouds they were flying over.

As he leaned back, coffee in hand, he thought *man, how did I get here*? Never in his wildest dreams did he imagine himself on a luxury private jet, flying off to Panama, married to a woman who..., well, there was just no way to describe his wife. As he sipped his coffee, his mind wandered back to how his life had once been, and what he had always wanted: a home, a wife, and someday a family. Well, he had two out of three, but his home life was far from normal. Could he live with that? Did he want to live with that? He knew the answer as soon as he looked out the window again. Flying high, that's what his marriage was, flying high above the clouds. It wasn't traditional for sure, but then again, he wasn't like everyone else either. The one thing he knew for sure was that Addie's love for him meant more than he could ever put into words. He knew that no matter where this life took them, or where they would end up, he was going to be with Addie. He would follow her to the ends of the earth. If she'd let him.

"Hey Martin, are you awake?" Nick asked.

"I am," Martin answered, "and buckled up just like you instructed. What's going on? How come it's going to be a rough landing? It doesn't look like bad weather."

"Nothing to do with the weather," Nick answered, plopping down in the chair across from Martin. The chair was so big and plush it looked like it was swallowing the boy. "Man, I love these chairs. I think their bigger than my bed at home. Anyway, it's the landing strip. Can you believe it's up on top of a mountain or something and hasn't had much traffic since Mr. Trask's died? Not to mention this is a bigger plane than they are used to landing there. Joe says it's no problem for him, so don't worry."

"I'm not worried, are you?"

"Nope, Addie only hires the best. I bet Joe can land any plane almost anywhere," Nick assured him.

"I bet you're right. Did Joe teach you anything besides how to use the intercom?"

"He did, he told me lots about Panama. Do you know there are all kinds of colored frogs, toucans, monkeys and sloths? Joe says we might get to see some of them. He said Mr. Trask loved birds and had lots of them come by the compound courtyard because he fed them. Isn't that an awful thing to call your house, a compound? I guess it's like an old fortress or something super cool. Where's everyone else?" Nick asked.

"In conference, a fortress? Hmm, you think we'll find any ghosts there?" Martin asked.

"I'm sure we will. Mr. Trask died in a car accident, but Joe said it wasn't too far from there and he said Mr. Trask loved that house so much. Do you think he's still there, Martin? Do you think he'll talk to Addie? That would be way cool," Nick said, leaning forward.

"It sure would be cool and if it was an old fortress, it might have had a jail or even a dungeon," Martin said.

"Maybe it does. Who knows, maybe Mr. Trask knew how to torture people. He was pretty high up in the Secret Service you know."

"That he was. Hey, how about we play a game? Martin said, picking up a deck of cards that were lying on the table.

"Five card stud?" Nick answered, raising his eyebrows.

"Works for me," Martin said, and began shuffling the cards.

"No time to play now," They heard Ray say as the door to the conference room opened and the team started to file out.

"You need us?" Nick asked, sitting up straight in his chair.

"Young man, this is called a need-to-know briefing," Ray answered, taking the chair next to Nick's.

Holly and Addie were the last ones out. Holly tapped a button on her pad as they watched a panel on the wall slid up, revealing a holographic model of the layout of their destination.

"Wow, look at that," Nick said.

"Wow is right," Bird answered.

"It looks like we're there," said Nick, standing to get a closer look.

"Stay in your chair Nick and buckle up," Holly said, "I'll bring it to you," Nick watched as Holly sat and buckled up. "We'll be landing soon," They watched as Holly quickly moved her fingers along the screen of her pad. As she did this, the landscape increased in size to fill the entire room.

"Is that better?" Holly asked.

"Unbelievable is more like it," said Bat.

"The boys in the toy room are geniuses," Holly answered, "then again, Addie and the founders only hire the best of the best.

"What are we looking at? Does this belong to us, or is it something we're planning on taking?" Bird asked.

"What you see is the compound of our Founder, Pavel Trask. It was designed by him and built by a handpicked group of men that all worked for Solomon Inc." Addie started to explain. "For those of you that never worked with him, let me give you some background. Trask's official title when he retired was Special Agent Director of the Secret Service. He was the first person recruited by the pentagon to head Project W.I.S.E. He recruited his old college buddy, Isaac McClellan, who was a retired Admiral of the United States Navy. Trask never married and there are no known children. The reason that is important is because Solomon Inc. was named as his sole heir."

20

"So, what you're saying is, all of this now belongs to the company?" Bat asked.

"Exactly," They heard Snoop's voice answer.

"Even though it's not in Panama City, we will be using the compound as our base of operation. We'll be landing here," Addie said, pointing to an airstrip on the top of a plateau, which was about a mile from the compound.

"I don't see a hanger. Addie, you aren't planning on just letting our beautiful girl sit out on the top of a mountain for anyone to see...," Ray asked, patting the arm of his chair.

"Or blow up," said Bat.

"You'll see when we land why we don't need a hanger to protect the Queen of Sheba," Addie answered smiling.

"I can't wait to see what Trask did with the place. He used me as a consultant several years on some plans for a meditation room," Pike said.

"I heard he spent more money than all of the other Partners combined just on this compound alone. What was it Addie, over sixty million?" Angus asked.

"More like one hundred and fifty million. After that, I stopped counting. He always used to say that we had to remember the price included the furnishings and his impressive and extensive wine and spirit cellar," Addie answered.

"Which, as I recall, is bigger than most liquor stores," Dusty added.

"With wine and spirits so rare, you can only find them for sale by collectors and then you have to know how to contact the collector," Pike answered.

"As I understand it, the only room that's bigger than the wine cellar is his armory. I've never been shown the entire house, so I'm trusting Snoop to guide us through it using this new holographic technology," Addie said, waving her hand over the images they were looking at.

"The main house looks like it's one story," said Dusty.

"It is, but in reality, it's Five. Four of the floors are completely underground," Addie explained.

"Wow, look at that, its elegance reminds me of some of the old houses in New Orleans. From the outside, they look like nothing but a shack but inside," Bat said.

"How many rooms are we talking about up top?" Bird asked.

"There are five bedrooms, one indoor and one outdoor kitchen. There is a game room with billiard tables, holographic gaming, and several collector chess tables. Then there is the smoking room, which comes complete with a built-in cigar closet that is connected to his below ground stash. It reminds me of the old dumbwaiters. Other rooms include Trask's library with adjoining offices, three lounging areas and a veranda. There are also several bars throughout the house," Holly explained, while virtually moving the team around the house. The holographic program was so technically advanced that it made them all feel as though they were actually walking around the house.

"The man knew how to live in more ways than one," Pike told them. "I would say he forgot more than most people will ever know and could converse on almost any subject. As a matter of fact, I can't think of a subject he didn't know at least something about. If the situation ever arose that he actually didn't know something, you could bet that he would do some research and find out all about it within twenty-four hours. Everyone used to call him the sponge."

Before Holly could continue, Joe was instructing everyone to shut off the equipment. As the plane descended through the clouds, Nick and Martin opened the shades and started to see the lush green land below them. As they watched, the plane seemed to be heading straight for the top of a mountain.

As they turned to make their final decent, they could see the runway. It looked exactly like the holographic image had shown; only it was just a runway with no buildings. A couple of bumps later, they watched Joe turn the plane and drive it back to the center of the runway. He stopped in the middle of what looked like a giant target.

"Please, everyone remain seated and buckled in until I give you the all-clear," They heard Joe say. The second he finished his instructions, there was a loud scrapping sound, followed by a sinking feeling. Those that were sitting near the windows stared silently in disbelief.

"The runway is falling into the mountain!" Nick screeched, "Addie, we're going to die!"

"Not so fast little solider, no one dies on my watch," said Ray, grabbing hold of Nick to calm him down. Thankfully, it worked. Ray felt the boy relax and his face softened.

"Don't worry Nick, we're fine. Remember, there weren't any hangers up top. This is a new plane and I can't let it sit outside. Also, we don't want to make it easy for our enemies to find us," Addie explained.

There was a thud and the platform came to a stop.

"Please remain seated and buckled in until the doors open," Joe's voice said over the intercom.

"Man, he sounds like those pilots on TV," Nick said.

"He actually used to be a commercial pilot before Addie took him away from all that," Debbie told him.

"I'm still hoping that I can steal his wife too," Addie said, looking over at Debbie who was smiling back. They all turned as Joe opened the doors and walked into the conference area.

"We're ready to deplane," Joe announced. Addie heard Snoop's voice in her ear bud as she unbuckled her seatbelt.

"Alarms are set Addie. If I see anything, I'll let you know. Please keep your ear piece in," Snoop said.

"Will do any sign of visitors?" Addie asked.

"None so far, hey, was Henry ever down here?" Snoop asked.

"Not officially. Trask was very clear about that. Henry was never to be at any of the meetings here or in Minneapolis. Both he and Isaac were very clear that Henry and Ellis were to have limited contact."

"But Ellis was here many times. I know Trask ran transport cases through Panama and that was one of Ellis's specialties," said Snoop.

"Yes, but Ellis did all his work though the office in Panama City. To my knowledge, he didn't know the location of the compound. The only operatives that knew about this location were handpicked by Trask. Myself, Jacob, Pike and I believe he brought you down, is that correct Angus?" Addie asked. "Wasn't it to authenticate some rare documents he had purchased?"

"Yes, it was, my dear. However, I also spent many hours here working with Mr. Trask. I take it he didn't tell you about that?" Everyone looked at Angus, surprised he had been down here more than once.

"You're right about that Angus, I had no idea. Can I ask what you were working on?"

"You may, we were working on the boardroom," Angus answered as though it should be obvious.

"The board of directors needed a special room, one that he needed your help with? Angus, forgive me, but you can't even pound a nail in the wall to hang a picture without hurting yourself," Addie joked.

"For your information, I've gotten much better with tools, but that is not the kind of help Trask required from me. You'll see when the time comes."

Addie smiled back at him, still laughing at the very thought of Angus building anything.

"Just a reminder, everyone please keep your ear buds in at all times," They heard Snoop say. Suddenly, everyone's ear buds went dead, except for Addie's.

"Holly, go ahead and take the group down, I'll meet you on the runway," Addie told them. Holly nodded and led the way out of the plane. Addie told Martin to go ahead she needed to talk to Snoop in private. As he left her to join the group, he heard Addie say.

"They don't call you Snoop for nothing."

"You should know by now, Boss. I listen, watch, and basically butt in whenever I please. By the way, Jacob and Wolff are down below, exploring the private liquor vault. I saw them enjoying some of Trask's collection of Armagnac and puffing on cigars like they're Tony Montana, while pointing out each other's tells while their playing poker."

"Seriously? Don't tell them we're here yet. I want to take the group on a tour and we'll save the vault for last. By the way, who's winning the poker game?" Addie asked.

"Oddly enough Wolff, he's pointed out some interesting facial tells of Jacob's. Jacob is good too, but Wolff seems to be able to read him almost every single time," Snoop answered, sounding genuinely surprised.

"That's because Jacob is trained to read the faces of his target, but since he's the watcher, he doesn't have to be aware of his own tells. Although, knowing Jacob, he's taking it all in like a sponge and learning a lot about Wolff. Jacob is baiting Wolff and very soon, he will snap the trap," said Addie.

"Your usually right, Boss."

"Well, you could be right too. Do you want to place a little bet?" Addie asked.

"Sure, a hundred says Wolff takes him," Snoop answered.

"You're on. We'll see when we get there. And Snoop, no cheating," said Addie.

"Me? Cheat? How could I?" Snoop asked as innocently as he could muster.

"By telling Wolff what Jacob's hand is, obviously," Addie shot back. She turned and started to head down to meet up with her team. In the meantime, Holly had continued with the holograph tour of the floors below the compound.

"Hey Boss, I'm shocked that you would suggest such a thing. You have my word, no cheating, being the pure sportsman that I am. I'll even let you listen to the feeds if you like," Snoop told her.

"I trust you Snoop being the sportsman that you are, and it's only a hundred," Addie said while rejoining the group.

CHAPTER 4

"Jacob, if you're playing with me," Wolff said. He walked over to the tasting table and picked up the decanter of Armagnac they'd been drinking from. As he lifted the decanter, he noticed the strange shapes and markings on the stand that held the decanter.

"Jacob, have you ever looked at this stand?" Wolff asked. He picked it up and looked at the bottom. It had strange loops and circling metal pieces that came together around a main circle, which formed small legs that were holding a porcelain tray.

"Unique, same as all the objects Trask collected. Everything in this house was a passion of his. The liquor, cigars, do you know why the top of this poker table is so soft?" Jacob asked.

"No, why?" Wolff asked.

"Because it's not felt, it's deer skin that was made especially for this table."

"Seriously? Why would anyone want a deer skin covered poker table?" Wolff asked. He was still looking at the symbol that formed the legs of the stand as he took a sip of the dark brown liquid. "I've seen this design before somewhere, I just can't remember where."

"You've had too much Armagnac. You better go slow on that man, you're not used to the good stuff. Or maybe you're just stalling," Jacob teased.

Wolff set the stand back down on the table, pounded down the rest of his drink and poured another one, before replacing the decanter and walking back to the table.

"Are you going to play poker or drink?" Jacob asked, tapping his cards.

"What's the matter Jacob, haven't lost enough yet?" Wolff asked.

27

"Respect the game and play," Jacob said. He sat back and took a long drag on his cigar. The tobacco was so dark it was black. The flavor was an absolute testament to the cigar closet Trask had custom built, they were fairly old but still tasted amazingly fresh.

"Read them and weep," Declared Wolff, as he showed his full house to Jacob.

"Wow, would you look at that hand. Lady Luck must follow you, just like all the ladies do, or used to anyway," said Jacob. He laid down a Royal Flush, took another puff of his cigar and leaned in to wipe the pot off the table.

"You were playing me. I ought to..."

"Ought to what? Man, I had to wait until the pot got big enough to make it worth my while. Wolff, old man, you are a pleasure to play with," Jacob said smiling.

"You were purposely playing with those tells, you knew I'd be watching your every move and you played it up," Wolff said. "Well played Jacob. I can't say it's been a pleasure, but it is a..."

"Jacob, you old goat," Bird's voice rang out from the doorway to the cellar, just as Wolff moved to shake Jacob's hand.

"Bird? Man, it's been a long time and you're just as ugly as ever. What's your good-looking woman Bat up to these days?" Jacob asked, standing to shake hands and hug his old friend.

"I'm not his woman and I'm up to no good. How are you Jacob?" Bat asked, coming over to hug him and kiss his cheek.

"If you aren't his woman, then you can do better than that," Jacob said, pulling her close and kissing her hard.

"Not in front of the children," Jacob heard Bird say. Releasing Bat, he looked past Wolff to see the room filling fast, led by Addie.

Addie smiled as Jacob released Bat. "Don't mind us," said Addie.

"What do you mean, don't mind *us*? I don't know who this guy is, but he's kissing Bat and he didn't even ask permission, not to mention the germs, yuck," Nick said, stepping forward.

"You hiring kids now Addie? What's the matter, you run out of cast offs from Uncle Sam?" Jacob asked.

"Hey, I'm no kid. I'm Nick, operative in training, you can ask Master Tan," Nick retorted. He then walked over to stand in front of Jacob, his feet firmly planted and his hands on his hips.

Jacob dropped his arm from around Bat's waist and stepped up to face Nick. "Kid, did you say Tan is your master?"

Nick stepped closer and looked straight up at Jacob. "He is, and so is Wolff here, and I told you my name is Nick, not kid."

"So, you did, Nick it is. You must be good if both Tan and Wolff agreed to train you," Jacob said, holding his hand out to Nick.

Nick hesitated, looked back at Wolff who nodded back, then took hold of Jacobs hand and shook it hard with a grip that surprised the older man. Wolff smiled back at Jacob, thinking that this must be what it's like to have a son that just quarterbacked the winning team. The feeling surprised the tough man. Wolff always prided himself in being a lone wolf with no strings attached, and certainly no ties to his heart.

"If we can put a lid on all the testosterone in the room, maybe we can get down to introductions, have a drink and make a plan?" Addie said.

"We can," Jacob said, pulling out a chair for Bat. Bird took Jacob's chair next to Bat. "Bird, you would deprive an old friend the pleasure of sitting next to your lovely lady?"

"You forget Jacob I've known you longer than Bat has I have been a firsthand witness to how you treat the ladies," Bird said, pulling out the chair next to him for Jacob. Jacob smiled, graciously accepted the chair, and watched as the rest

29

of the team emerged from the shadows. They heard soft voices and bottles tinkling from further back in the vault. There was a cheer from behind one of the racks.

"That you Ray?" Wolff called out.

"It is, you old dog. I'm with your lady and we are having some great wine. Trask only housed the best," Ray answered. He and Holly emerged carrying a case of wine.

"Girl, they let you out again? And for your information Ray, Holly is not my lady," Wolff said.

"I can speak for myself, Mr. Wolff," Holly retorted.

"Good to know," Ray said. "She's been indispensable to us. I can't wait until this job is done so she can come back to New Orleans for some well-deserved down time," He said, smiling over at Wolff.

"Madam, please, take my chair," Jacob said. Standing, he started walking towards Holly.

"Mr. Jacob, is it? Thank you for offering, but its better if I stand so I can operate the program efficiently," said Holly. She was staring at her pad, but started moving closer to this handsome man, smiling at him sweetly.

She turned to see Ray and Pike pouring wine and handing out glasses. She slipped her pad under her arm and accepted a glass. Lifting it to her nose, she took a deep breath and was amazed by the aroma. She knew the wine was very old, but the aroma from the grapes was fresh and light, like they had just been picked.

"Wonderful, isn't it?" She heard Jacob whisper.

"Does it taste as good as it smells?" She asked.

"All of Trask's possessions were the very best. He would settle for nothing less. He always said he didn't have to."

"He didn't. He had the Wisdom of Solomon and knew how to use it," Angus explained.

"Please, everyone, let's get on with the introductions and see if we can come up with a plan," Addie instructed. She motioned everyone to follow her to the tasting room. It was a separate room within another small cavern. There was a long table that went down the middle of the room with a clean, white linen tablecloth that appeared to have been recently laid.

"How is it so clean? Hasn't this been here for a long time? Didn't you say Trask died a couple of years ago?" Debbie asked Joe as they followed the others into the room.

"I can answer that," said Jacob. "Trask died over three years ago. As for this room, the air down here is expertly filtered, and the temperature is controlled, so there is no dust, mold, or mildew. Trask also provided for housekeeping to continue, which was one thing I didn't fully understand, but maybe now I do," He said. Jacob reached down and ran his fingers across the linen.

"Please, everyone be seated and let's get started," Addie said. She took Trask's chair at the head of the table and motioned for Wolff to take the chair to her right. Addie then motioned for Martin to take the chair to her left, much to everyone's surprise, including Wolff's. Addie remained standing while the rest were seated. Before she took her seat, she gave a toast in ancient Aramaic. Angus translated, "To Wisdom and her Abundance. And to the three who knew her past and future."

Jacob lifted his glass and said, "To the Founders, and those they passed the torch to." They all lifted their glasses and took a drink in silence.

CHAPTER 5

Wolff broke the silence first. "Addie, what do you say we finish this thing, whatever it is?"

"I agree. Wolff, we'll start with you and go around the table. Everyone state your name and specialty," Addie instructed.

"Wolff, my specialties include: intelligence, recon, tactical planning, munitions and hand-to-hand combat," Wolff said.

"Pike, tactical backup, sniper, physicist and historical expert."

"Angus, historian, linguist, theological anthropologist and demonologist."

"Joe, pilot."

"Debbie, assistant to Angus and whatever Addie and Holly need me to do."

"Ray, tactical equipment design, team command, personnel protection, firearms and demolition expert."

"Holly, communications and field operations coordinator."

"Dusty, transport, if it can be driven it, I'm your man."

"Jacob, sniper."

"Austin, ex-Navy seal from New Orleans, bodyguard to Addie, that now includes Martin and Nick."

"Snoop, toys, communications, infiltration logistics and anything else Addie can come up with."

"Bird, Army special forces we were called tactical ghost soldiers."

"Bat, Army intelligence, communications and medic."

"Nick, anything anyone asks me to do," The entire team couldn't help but laugh. Nick looked over at Addie with a solemn look on his face.

"Nick and Martin will be considered operative's in training. From what Tan tells me, my husband shows aptitude in several areas in our line of work. Also, I haven't found anything that he can't repair."

"What has Tan been training them to do?" Snoop asked.

"Firearms, demolition, hand-to-hand combat and surveillance," Martin answered.

"Great, how about Nick?" Snoop asked.

Nick looked over at Addie.

"Hey boy, answer the man," Austin said, poking Nicks shoulder from behind.

Wolff was on his feet, glaring across the table at Austin. "Let's get one thing straight. From now until this job is done, Nick is every bit an operative and a member of our team. He may be the youngest, and still in training, but he is no *boy*. Do I make myself clear?"

To everyone's surprise, Addie did not intervene or disagree.

"You do, Mr. Wolff. Nick, you have the floor," Austin said. He was backing away, but never took his eyes off Wolff.

Wolff sat down and nodded to Nick. Nick cleared his throat before he spoke.

"I've been in training with Martin. Master Tan says I'm really good at hand-to-hand combat and surveillance because I'm good at thinking at least three moves ahead. I told him I learned that by playing chess with grandpa, and because I pay attention to detail. I have a good memory too."

"Thank you all. In a minute, Holly will go over your assignments, but before she starts I want to go over a couple of things. First of all, I think you all know that we believe both Trask and Isaac did not die of natural causes. Do we all agree?" Everyone around the room nodded.

"Second of all, I believe most of you in this room are familiar with at least some of the details surrounding the original Solomon project and the founding of this corporation by Retired Admiral, Isaac McClellan, and Retired Special Agent Director of Secret Service, Pavel

Trask. So, for some of you, this will be old news and I'm sorry for that. However, I feel that we need to go over it with everyone in order to decide on our tactical plan. From time to time, I may be asking some of you to fill in some of the pieces that I'm unaware of, and at any time please feel free to interrupt," said Addie. They all got comfortable in their chairs, knowing that this would take a while.

"Good, let's get started everyone. Snoop and Holly will bring up holographic documents and details as we need them. Snoop, as you were one of the first members, would you start?" Addie asked.

"Yes Ma'am. I was one of the original operatives that was hired by Isaac and Trask. We were all hired separately, and none of us knew about any of the others until we finally worked together on a project. Since I handled all the communications, I was assigned to stay in contact with everyone."

"I also act as an archivist for Solomon Inc. The search for Solomon's wisdom has been sought by men since its supposed disappearance with the great king himself. Originally undiscovered documents and testing reports were found in Germany after World War II. Our government reviewed them, decided they were of no value and archived them until some intelligence came across the desk of Retired Army General, Henry Perrin.

He had always been interested in what he called *the folklore* surrounding the Wisdom of Solomon. The information he found led him back to the archives. He pulled the material and started to compare it with the current information. He thought he could succeed where the others had failed. He took his proposal to the powers that be and the Project W.I.S.E was born. The rest is history, as they say."

"Henry handpicked Isaac and Trask, his cross functional team, from the Navy and Secret Service. Together, they picked all of us and we were called The First Team. We were all still active military at the time, all except for Marie.

Henry assigned her to be the trainer on matters *of the other side,* is how he described her."

"We were all separated from each other and we only came together as a team when we had to, but none of us really knew much of anything. It was Henry, Trask and Isaac that studied with Marie. At least, that's what I could find out. Then one day, suddenly, it all fell apart. One by one we were called in by Henry. Oh, and prior to that day, we never had any contact with Henry. He told us that the project was being shut down and that Trask and Isaac were retiring. I was told that I was being sent back to my ship, back to regular duty for the U.S. Navy. But after working on the Project, there was just no way that I could go back to being a regular Navy," Snoop said.

"I remember the day I was called in by Henry. Similar to Snoop, I was an active member of the U.S. Army. We were just starting to make real progress and every mission was a success, even though they were getting harder and more complicated. Trask and Isaac always seemed to pull together the right team for every job and the plans were intricate but always spot on. We never lost," Ray said, pinching his forehead between his fingers.

"Yeah, well at least you guys still had a job to go back to. They didn't bother to offer me the option to stay because they thought I knew too much. Hell, I didn't know anything," Jacob said.

"Trask told me to be on guard, that he would be out of contact for a while, but he had a plan. Little did I know, it was almost dawn when I heard them coming. In order to save my own life, I was forced to kill two men before coffee."

"What did you do?" Nick asked hanging on to Jacob's every word.

"I went underground and found Trask. He was the one that had brought me into the project. Now, by God, he was

35

going to tell me what he'd gotten me into and why Uncle Sam was trying to kill me,"

"Did he tell you?" Debbie asked.

"No, not then what he did was bring me here to join the new team he was building. I was his personal operative until the day he was murdered," Jacob said.

"Don't you mean until he was killed in a car accident?" Asked Holly.

"Girl, the longer you know me, you'll start to realize that I always mean what I say. I will not rest until I prove that Trask was murdered," Jacob snapped.

"We will prove it, together Jacob. While we're at it, we will also prove who killed Isaac and find out why Uncle Sam is so interested in a project he dumped," Addie said.

"I remember the day Trask showed up at my house. Among other things, that man was the master of disguises, I didn't even recognize him. I thought he was just an old man walking along the hillside lane, leaning on a walking stick, which was much taller than him I might add. The only clue I had was when my dog, instead of his usual barking, was whining to be let out. That indicated to me that someone he knew was outside and he wanted to say hello. To be safe, I pulled my gun and opened the door. Zeus, my dog, ran straight for the old man. At first, I was afraid he was going to knock him over, but then I heard that strong voice of Trask's say, *'I can't fool you, can I old boy?'* Then he told me to invite him in and take him to my office. He knew that he could not be detected in my house," Pike said.

"So, you four are the only ones left from the original Solomon project?" Debbie asked.

"Oh, I am sure there were others, but we don't know them. We didn't find out about each other until Trask brought us together. Trask was our handler. We never knew who Isaac and Henry were handling. The only time I heard anything, was one time when Trask told me to watch out for an operative that Henry had been grooming, they called him…," Ray answered.

"Bright Star," Interrupted Jacob.

"Yeah, that's right," said Ray, surprised that Jacob also knew that name.

"Well, we don't have to worry about him, I killed him and this handler," Jacob said.

"What are you talking about?" Asked Ray.

"Ray, I don't normally kill and tell, you know that," Jacob said smiling.

"We will talk about that later," said Addie, "So other than this guy Bright Star, the only ones we all know of from the original project are the four of you."

"So, where do we go from here?" Bird asked.

"For starters, we find Trask's private office and hopefully find some answers there," Addie said.

"Well, I can show you where his office is, but getting in is going to be another thing," said Jacob, standing.

"You know where Trask's office is?" Wolff asked.

"Sure, I was the operative in charge of the project when it was being built, and I was assigned to oversee the men who were building it," Jacob answered.

"So, what are we waiting for? Lead on, man," Wolff said standing.

They watched as Jacob stood and walked over to the opposite side of the room to a wall that was covered in photos, some of which were Trask's favorite places. Walking to the far left, almost to the back wall of the cavern, was a smaller photo of a vineyard with rolling hills. The picture had been taken at sunset and was absolutely breathtaking.

"Cognac France," said Jacob. He tilted the picture clockwise and they all watched in amazement as the wall slid away to the right. This revealed a set of double metal doors that each spanned at least two feet wide.

"Of course, it would be Cognac that opened the door," Wolff said smiling.

"It did not open the door it just opened the wall that exposed the door. I have no idea where the key is," Jacob said, moving aside to let others get a closer look.

"I thought you said you were in charge of building it?" Demanded Wolff.

"Overseeing it being built, I never said that I had access to it," Jacob shot back.

"Calm down boys. Snoop, do you know anything about this door?" asked Addie.

"I know about the lock, but I don't know about the key. There is only one type of lock that is impenetrable, even by explosive, and guess which type of lock this is. I'm also not sure that the rest of the wall doesn't have some kind of fail-safe that would destroy the office should someone try to enter it without the key," Snoop answered.

"The doors come together flush, and I don't see a keyhole anywhere, only a keypad," Pike said.

"Right you are, I'm sure several of you know the code, you just don't know you know," Snoop said.

"I love games," said Angus, from the back of the group.

"I don't," Wolff said, looking over at Holly.

"Angus, who was the demon that was defeated by God's angel in the book of Tobit, also known as the book of Tobias?" Snoop asked.

"Trask, you sly old boy, I know both answers," Angus squealed. He sounded like a little boy on Christmas morning.

"Okay, first type in the name of the demon wait for the first part of the lock to be revealed and then type in the Angel's name. The lock will accept the code for twenty-four hours. After that, if you don't find the key, the keyhole will reset with new clues over the next seven days," Snoop told them.

"God, that man loved his games," said Jacob.

"Yeah, that's why I never liked him, I hate games," Wolff said.

38

"And you're not very good at them either," Jacob answered. Wolff shot him a dirty look.

"The number seven is the foundation of God's word. It is the number of completeness and perfection, since it's tied to God's creation of all things," Pike said. Everyone turned to look at him. "Sorry, I was just thinking out loud."

"And there are at least seven men in the Old Testament who are specifically mentioned as men of God," said Angus.

"Is Solomon one of them?" Holly asked.

"No, but his father, David, was," Debbie answered.

"Excellent, you are so right dear lady," Angus said, clapping his hands for her.

"Calm down Angus, don't hurt yourself. First things first, if you get the answers typed in correctly, we may not need the seven-day thing," said Wolff. Looking over at Holly, he noticed that both Jacob and Ray had come behind her and were looking over her shoulder at something on her pad, while whispering in her ear. Wolff felt his cheeks flush. *Push it down, push it down, you don't have time for a woman, you have a job to do*, he kept telling himself. He had to admit that he couldn't stand watching the other men being that close to her. Damn, was he in love with Holly? He shook his head and tried to put it out of his mind. No, he couldn't be, not him.

CHAPTER 6

Angus approached the keypad. Before he started to type, he turned back to Pike. "What do you think Pike, do you think he would put in the English translation?"

"Snoop, do we only get so many tries?" Asked Pike.

"As far as I know. Remember, Trask was multilingual and I think he was up to eleven languages; Greek and Aramaic were two of them."

"Alright, so first we try English and move on from there. I guess we'll just have to see how much the old boy wanted to play with us," Angus said, starting to press keys. He entered the first name and stopped. There was a whirring sound and a panel opened on one door, revealing half of what must be the keyhole. "So far so good, and now we know that the demon is first and the angel is second," He said, stepping forward to type in the angel's name.

"Why would that be important?" Wolff asked him.

"I don't know yet, but in the book of Tobit he was on the scene for pretty much the whole book. Let's see if it works," Angus muttered. Next, he typed in the Archangel's name, Raphael. This time, on the other door directly opposite the first, a lighted panel appeared, revealing the second half of the keyhole.

"What in the world is that?" Asked Angus.

"It's huge," Holly noted.

"So where do we start looking for a key that size?" Debbie asked.

"He would have left it somewhere close by and in plain sight," offered Dusty.

"I agree, so let's start looking," Addie said.

"Addie, have you thought of asking Trask?" Asked Pike.

"No, it's forbidden to call forth a spirit," Addie told the group.

"Is it forbidden to ask if he'd like to join us for a drink?" Martin asked.

"I could do that. Holly, please put the digital recorder on. Snoop, let's try it from your end too," Addie instructed.

"You got it Boss," Both Holly and Snoop said in unison.

"Great minds think alike," said Martin. "Addie, what do you need us to do?"

"Let's all sit around the table. Whoever sits at the head of the table can open," They all did as they were told and sat down. Addie walked to the sideboard along one of the long cavern walls and chose a cut-glass tumbler, which was very ornate and yet very masculine. "I remember Trask using these glasses when he had an evening..." Suddenly the air in the room stirred and the temperature dropped.

"Holly, please record EMF and temperature readings," Instructed Addie.

"There was a spike in EMF and the temperature has dropped three degrees," Holly answered.

"Come on Trask, you can do better than that. Should I put out a flashlight for you to play with?" Addie joked. Before she could say anything else, a glass lifted off the shelf, hovered in mid-air and then smashed to the floor. Everyone jumped and Holly let out a little gasp.

"Touché Trask, no sense of humor, always working, always so serious. Here, let me pour you a drink and we can talk," Addie said, walking out of the cavern room and into the main cellar.

"She's advanced, she's as good as Trask was or maybe even better," Jacob said, looking between Martin and Wolff.

"No, she's far more advanced than the founders ever were, she's a doorway to the other side," Angus told them. The whole room turned to look at him.

"What do you mean by that?" Martin asked.

"Guys, the temperature is back up four degrees," Holly said.

41

"He's with her, what I meant is, that Addie walks with one foot in this dimension and one foot in the other. She seems to be able to go back and forth at will. She talks about eating and drinking with them on their side. She is the most advanced person I have ever seen," Angus explained.

"Since Bright Star," Pike added.

Addie couldn't hear them she was in the cellar trying to make contact with Trask or whoever was there with her. She walked over to the serving chest and put a glass down next to the stand that was holding the decanter. Carefully, she picked up the beautiful cut-glass decanter of dark brown liquid. Lifting her nose as she removed the stopper, she opened her mouth slightly and took a slow breath in. As she swirled the liquid around, she let the scent of the expensive Armagnac roll around her senses the way Trask had taught her. She recognized the rich smells as one of her favorites, but not one of Trask's. The decanter must have been almost full, since she knew the boys had been drinking from it.

She took one more deep breath and as she did, the area around her grew frigid. The cold went around her like someone was putting their arms around her waist. Next, she felt the cold hit her shoulder as the soft voice of Trask whispered in her ear. She knew it was him when he called her by the pet name he'd given her.

"Sweet, I see you remembered your lessons, how not to summon but to tease. You also remembered how to breathe in the Armagnac and prepare your pallet for the first sip," She heard him whisper.

"I remembered Sir. You and your lessons are hard to forget," Addie answered, now completely chilled to the bone.

"I am Sweet, and my memory is intact. At least I hope I remembered right, this Armagnac was your favorite, but not mine, correct?" Trask asked.

"You are correct Sir. Would you like me to pour you a glass anyway?" Addie asked, her teeth chattering.

"Heavens no, follow me," Addie felt the cold leave her. As she watched, a light blue mist formed a pillar in front of her and started moving to cabinet against one of the cavern walls. It came to a stop next to one of the glass doors and a thin trail of mist reached for the knob of the cabinet.

"Sir, please allow me," Addie said. As she moved to the cupboard, the mist moved to the side and she could see an outline starting to form. Trask now stood beside her and looked exactly as he had the last time they'd been together.

He pointed as he spoke, "There, the rounded bottle on the second shelf. No Sweet, the one next to it."

"Sir, this is one of your one hundred-year-old Armagnac's. Are you sure you want me to open it?" Addie asked.

"Sweet, I'm dead and you hardly ever drink, of course I want you to open it. Besides, you're not the only one that can create something from nothing. You'll find the proper glasses in the bottom of the cabinet," Trask said. He turned, walked to the nearest poker table, and sat down. Addie joined him with the glasses in one hand and the unopened bottle in the other. He motioned for her to set the glasses down on the table, which surprised her, knowing what they were made of and how fussy Trask had always been. She decided to verify that this really was her old friend.

"Sir, I'll need you to state your full name for me. I need to verify your identity," Addie stated in a very stern voice.

"Are you out of your mind? You invade my house and when I do you the honor, and I do mean the absolute honor of communicating with you...," The spirit spat at her.

Without flinching Addie demanded again. "Spirit, state your full name, in the name of Jesus I command it."

The spirit swelled and the light blue tint turned first to a deep amethyst, then to a deep wine and last to crimson. "You dare defy me," It bellowed at her, rising and moving toward her. Addie simply held up her hand, repeated her demand and waited. The mist was now red and pulsing, swirling

43

around her and seemed to be dispersing. Finally, in a voice that reverberated through the cavern, he said, "I am Destracción and you are mine," The voice swirled all around her.

"I am a child of Yahweh and I banish you from this place. I shut your uttering's and I bind you from all the people covered by my favor forever in the name of Yahweh. Be gone now, before I bind you from the earth for all of eternity," Addie's voice was stern, but incredibly calm. As she commanded, she waved her hand in front of her as if fanning smoke from a fire. The mist was silent as she walked through it and turned to see it growing smaller.

"You have no right over me," The voice bellowed back at her, this time much more respectful and quiet.

"Destracción, I play no games. I claim no right over you, I only claim dominion. Now be gone before I bind you further," Addie spat back. Immediately there was a cry of torment emanating from the red smoke as it dropped down through the floor.

Addie stayed where she was for a moment then walked to the table where she had left the bottle and glasses, and poured herself a drink.

With her free hand, she let her fingers slide over the dark green deer skin that covered the table. Addie sat down and had just gotten comfortable when she heard Trask's unmistakable voice behind her. She was so tired from her encounter with the spirit that she didn't even turnaround in her chair. She simply asked, "Spirit, I command you in the name of the Lord Jesus Christ to tell me your full name,"

"My name is Pavel Nathanial Trask, Retired Special Agent Director of Secret Service. How dare that son of a snake use the pet name I gave you. By the way Sweet, when did you know it wasn't me?" Trask asked, walking over to sit opposite her. He carried a drink in one hand and a cigar in the other.

"Lots of things, but for one thing, you would have never let me open that bottle. Am I right Sir?"

"Right you are Sweet. I knew that serpent was here. I bumped into it a couple of times. I thought it was odd that it was here, so I sat back and watched. I didn't understand why it was here until...," Trask said smiling. It looked to Addie like he was looking at something behind her. Before she could turn around to see who it was, she heard the voice.

"Until I came?" Addie heard Isaac, her mentor and the second founding partner of Solomon Inc. Addie jumped up off her chair as he approached. Instinctively, she spread out her arms to hug him, but he put his hand up to stop her. She stopped short, remembering her training. She lifted her right hand and placed it against the outline of his upheld left hand. Her deep amethyst mingled with his yellow, forming a muddy looking color between them.

This was one of the first metaphysical games Marie had taught her. Decide what color light the two of you need as you come in contact with each other. Take the tones of color up or down to make the desired color.

"Addie girl, I want you to make our light a deep emerald, we need the power light. Bring your color to a cobalt blue as my yellow darkens. That's it, just a little deeper blue. Wonderful, now remember what this blue feels like. When you need to fight, you and your guardian will need to come together as one," Addie closed her eyes. The vibration was higher and a little more of an effort for her to hold, but she could do it. She opened her eyes to see him smiling back at her.

"Stop fooling around you two, we have work to do," They heard Trask say from behind them.

They dropped their hands and walked back to the table. Trask was lighting up a cigar that smelled just like the ones Jacob and Wolff had been smoking earlier. "By the way Addie, don't let anyone open my exclusive bottles, and it's a good thing it was Jacob who offered your man that cigar."

"Trask, Wolff is one of my best operatives and I have a feeling he might also be trainable. We need him for this job," Addie scolded.

"Addie, you're right. Trask just hates to admit it, he was really hoping it would be his boy Jacob," Isaac said. He sat down next to Addie and held up his hand. Addie watched as a wine glass appeared and filled itself. Isaac smiled at her and took a sip.

"Show off," Trask said. "Sweet, pour yourself a drink and let's get down to business."

"Yes, let's talk business I need to get back to my team," Addie said. She grabbed one of the glasses she had picked out earlier and poured herself a small amount of Armagnac from the decanter.

"You always did like the cut glass instead of the smooth swirls of my Tiffany glasses, as I remember," Trask commented.

"I like the way the cut glass plays with light, it reminds me of diamonds and you know how much I love my diamonds," Addie added. Opening her mouth, she breathed in the Armagnac, then took a sip and let it roll around on her tongue. She let it move from the front of her mouth to the back of her tongue, so she could taste as many of the ingredients and flavors as possible.

"Goodness woman, I do remember, you loved being paid in diamonds more than cold hard cash," Trask laughed.

"Sir, you ought to know by now, goodness had nothing to do with it," Addie answered, quoting Mae West. She finished the rest of her drink in one swallow. Putting the glass back down on the table, she looked Trask in the eye. "First things first, Sir, we need a key to your office."

"So maybe this will be your good man's first test," Trask said.

"That's not fair, he is not trained and we don't have time for your games," Addie countered.

Trask stood, looked down at her, and emptied his glass. He held up the glass as if he were about to give a toast, but couldn't because the contents of his glass disappeared. "Sweet, that's one thing you need to learn, there's always time for games. All of life is a game and its games that open the mind to infinite possibilities and imagination, which are the building blocks of reality."

"You had to get him started, didn't you?" Isaac said sighing.

"What do you want me to do?" Addie said. She shot an exasperated look over at Isaac, who sipped his wine and continued to look back and forth between the two of them, smiling.

"You? I don't want *you* to do anything. I will go find this dog of yours and see if he's as perceptive as you say," Trask answered.

"He's not my dog, his name is Wolff. He is no one's fool and I won't have you trying to make him one," Addie said standing.

"Don't get so upset. No one wants to make a fool of anyone. I will simply go to him, tell him where the key is and see if he has ears to hear me," Trask said.

"I'll go with him, Addie girl, and make sure he behaves. I think this will be a good test, you stay here and wait for us," Isaac told her.

CHAPTER 7

"Someone's coming," Wolff said. The others immediately stopped their conversations.

"I don't hear anything," Dusty said.

"I can," said Wolff again. Standing, he walked to the entrance next to Dusty.

"What do you hear? is it Addie coming back?" Pike and Angus asked at the same time.

"I hear what sounds like two men walking this way. They're wearing dress clothes and business shoes; the kind Ellis use to wear. I can hear them getting closer and talking to each other," Wolff said.

That's when the first motion sensor Dusty had planted (in the hallway leading to the wine tasting room) went off. "Gentlemen, something or someone is coming," Dusty said, pulling his gun. Holly stepped closer to them. Wolff put his arm out so that she would stay behind him and he pulled his gun.

Trask and Isaac stopped just outside the tasting room and looked over the group.

"Addie chose her team well," Isaac observed.

"Yes, our company started here in Panama and so did the corruption that's now threatening it," Trask said.

"Everyone, we have company," said Holly, "Snoop, are you seeing them?"

"I am, the temperature just dropped over eight degrees and the stick men are registering on my screen, how about yours Holly?" Snoop asked.

"I see them too. They are standing right in front of Wolff and the EMF coming from these two is over the top."

"Wolff, ask them who they are and then listen with your mind," Angus instructed.

"I can't do that, Addie's the one who talks to them," Wolff countered.

"Addie isn't here and from the looks of Holly's screen, they came to talk to you," Angus said.

"Maybe they have a message for Addie or maybe they came to show us where the key is," said Debbie, "Go ahead Wolff, try,"

"I don't know that lady, but her advice is sound and her light is very bright," Trask said to Isaac.

"She was a lady Addie worked with on one of our jobs. Turned out the perpetrator was a serial killer, of all things, that worked for a laboratory. He was an archivist. None of us could believe it," Isaac told Trask.

"Why not? It's always the quiet, secluded ones you need to worry about. They have too much alone time on their hands, which leads to bad thoughts. Did you ever find out why he was killing people?" Trask asked.

"Yes, it seems the people he killed were trying to doctor or hide testing values of prescription drugs. I didn't understand that part, but the short of it was, drugs were being released without reporting all the side effects. He killed the people that were responsible, to prevent them from putting any more dangerous drugs on the market. Very interesting case, you should read it sometime when this is over," Isaac told him.

"Well, I've got eternity," Trask said with a chuckle. "How do you want to start this?"

"Let me try, I've known Wolff since he first joined the military. I had Addie search him out in France and offer him a job with us. He's the one I met in Paris and told him where to find the book," Isaac explained.

Holly and Snoop watched on the monitor as one figures stepped closer to Wolff and seemed to put out a hand to shake.

"Wolff, one of them is very close to you and it looks like he's reaching out to shake your hand," Holly told him.

"Bat, do you know who this is?" Wolff pressed.

"No, for some reason I'm not being allowed to see, but I am not getting any bad vibes. In fact, I feel like I know them."

"What do I do?" Wolff asked Angus and Bat, who were now standing next to him.

"Put your hand out to shake his, take a deep breath and close your eyes. Ask him to tell you his name. The first time you make contact, it will be easier for him to put pictures in your mind, instead of you talking to him like Addie does. Don't be surprised if the pictures seem very real and you feel like you're actually there," Angus instructed.

"Don't be surprised if you feel like warm water is running over you," Bat added.

"What if I don't come back, like Bright Star?" Wolff asked.

"That is a totally different matter, Bright Star left his body, you are merely making contact," said Pike.

"Amazing," Debbie said.

Wolff took a deep breath, closed his eyes, and put out his hand. Immediately he felt a strong surge of energy go through him. This was accompanied by a sharp cold that felt like ice water going up his arm, across his shoulder, onto his cheek and finally settling on the side of his head. As soon as the cold reached his temple area, he saw them standing there. His old friend Isaac was holding his hand and Trask stood next to him holding a cigar.

"Isaac, it's you," Wolff said, "Man, it's so good to see you."

"Please, tell my man Jacob that I'm glad to see him, even though he gave you one of my cigars. I understand that he was just trying to be a good host. After all, this is his house now," said Trask.

"Jacob, Trask is here, he says it's good to see you. He was a little upset you gave me one of his cigars, but he accepts the fact that this is your house now," Wolff reiterated.

"Trask old man, I knew not even death could keep you down. But quit lying to my buddy, he takes things literally and gets all worked up. I gave him a cigar so that they wouldn't go to waste," Jacob said, moving closer to Wolff.

"All of you please beware of Henry. Find out what he's done, or is about to do, and stop him at all costs," said Trask.

"They will find out Trask, don't you worry about that. However, right now that's not the most important thing. You need to tell Wolff where to find the key," Isaac said.

"You tell him it's in the same place," Trask answered in a disgusted tone.

Isaac smiled at his old friend's response, it was true neither one of them had changed, personality wise that is. Even after death, they were still the same men they had always been. "Wolff, the key is on the bottom of the Armagnac decanter stand. Go get it, turn it over and insert it in the lock. Addie's retinal scan has been loaded in. Have her load in yours and Jacobs once you are in the office."

"Mr. Wolff, take all of your people in with you and lock the door. Don't come out until you or Addie hears from one of us. Do you understand?" warned Trask.

"Wolff, Addie knows how to get from the office to the store room without coming back out this way. There will be plenty there for all of you. We'll be in contact when it's time to make the next move. Tell Snoop and our Dear Holly that they will be able to play this entire conversation back, so that everyone will know you talked to us and what we said. Now go, and that's an order solider," Isaac said, smiling back at Wolff. Isaac suddenly realized that he couldn't break free of Wolff's grip. He had no idea this man was so strong in the light. Then, he saw her. Standing behind Wolff was a very petite, Native American woman. She looked straight at Isaac and said.

"My grandson has more to say," That's when Isaac saw that it was her energy going through Wolff's arm, gripping his hand. He also realized that she was blocking her presence from Wolff.

"Where is Addie?" Wolff asked. Isaac saw the old lady smile back at him.

"Waiting for you back in the poker room, she's long believed that you were trainable in the same way that she was. This is your first test solider, now move out," Isaac ordered.

CHAPTER 8

"Stay here, I'll be back with Addie," Wolff instructed. His tone made Holly huff, but he didn't hear her, his thoughts were on following his orders.

"He can hear and see them," Angus said to Pike.

"He can indeed, old friend."

"Who does he think he's giving orders to?" Holly muttered under her breath.

"The Boss he can give an order to any of us that he wants to give an order to," Jacob said sternly. "I never would have thought Wolff had it in him. For the first time ever, I'm actually jealous of the man."

"Don't be, Jacob. We all have our specialties and you are the best sniper I've ever known your instincts are just in a different form," Pike said, patting his shoulder.

"Holly, like it or not, can we count on you to take direction from Wolff the same way you would from Addie?" Pike asked. Every head in the room turned to look at Holly.

"Wolff?" Holly asked. "I still don't understand why Wolff would be in charge."

"Because he can walk in both worlds like Addie, and the rest of us can't. If anything should happen to Addie, Angus and I will be looking to him to lead. I'm sure when he comes back with Addie she will say more of the same," Pike answered.

"I'm a professional. I can and am willing to work with any member of this team, regardless of who the leader is," Holly stated.

"I know you are young lady, I just had to hear you say it because you're invaluable to this team, but only if you are working with us and not against us. I have a feeling that on this case, timing will be everything, our lives may depend on it," said Pike.

****

Wolff was silent. Every one of his nerves was on edge as he made his way back to the main cellar. He couldn't believe what had just happened. He never dreamed that he would inherit his grandmother's gift. The pictures of the games she used to play with him flashed in his mind as he made his way back. Once he arrived, Addie was waiting for him with a drink in her hand. He took it from her and drank it down. She hadn't forgotten his favorite whiskey.

"You okay with this?" Addie asked. She followed Wolff to the sampling table where he lifted the Armagnac from its stand. He set it down and picked up the stand, turning it over, he smiled.

"Wolff...," Addie pressed.

"Come on, we have to get back. I don't know if I'm okay with this. Hell no, I'm not okay, I don't want this, I never did," Wolff said. He didn't give her time to answer he just grabbed her arm and headed back to the tasting room.

"How long have you known?" Addie asked. She was running beside him to keep up.

"Since I was a child, at least my grandmother said I did. I never wanted to believe her, but I can't deny it anymore. I saw and heard them, just as clearly as I can see and hear you," Without warning, Wolff stopped abruptly. Addie ran into him.

"What the...," started Addie.

"Walk me through this Addie. Will you train me?" Wolff asked.

Addie touched his arm and smiled.

"Don't worry my friend, it's a gift, embrace it. You've always been a fast learner, and besides that, you're clearly a natural. Your Grandma said so and Grandmothers are never wrong, am I right?" Addie said. "Now, come on, the founders want us in the office. Something is up and I have a feeling that it's something that they can see or hear, but we can't," Addie didn't wait for him to grab her arm. This time, she was in the lead. Finally, the loan Wolff had found his connection or he finally admitted that it was real. She would work very hard to train him and hopefully, between her and the founders, they could talk him into taking Ellis's place as her partner. That is, if they survived the next round.

As they came around the corner of the cavern, Wolff called out to Dusty.

"I have the key get everyone to the door."

Addie let him take the lead. After all, he had the first part of the key. Besides, she wanted to see how he handled himself she loved watching her men in action.

Dusty had directed everyone to the door and then returned to his post at the front of the archway to the tasting room. Something wasn't right. He could feel it, but he couldn't see or hear anything.

Wolff moved along the side of the table and headed straight for the door. Addie, right behind him, smiled and nodded to the others reassuringly.

"I'll be dammed, the Armagnac stand. The old boy hid the key in plain sight and close enough so that he could get it anytime he wanted," Jacob said. Looking up toward the ceiling, he addressed his former Boss. "God, I miss you Trask, you old goat."

"Tell him that I'm right behind him," Trask told Addie. Addie didn't have to say a word, she could tell from across the room that Jacob felt the cold air around his shoulders. He shuttered and looked over at Addie, who was smiling back at him and winked.

The others didn't even notice, they were too busy watching Wolff. He turned the holder over, looked at the design, and matched it up to the lighted area on the lock. There was a sucking sound as the feet of the holder fell into place, but the door remained closed.

"What now?" Wolff asked, turning to Addie.

"Turn the knob like this," Addie said. Stepping forward, she grasped the edges of the stand like it was a safe handle. She turned it once to the right, once to the left, and then back to the center. They heard a low seductive male voice with an unmistakable southern drawl say.

"Welcome Addington, please step forward and let me look into your beautiful green eyes."

"Are you kidding me?" asked Wolff.

"It's obvious that Mr. Trask and Snoop are showing off their unique sense of humor," said Addie.

"Hey, don't blame me I only do as I'm told. Trask is the Boss," Snoop said into their ear buds.

Stepping forward, she let the retinal scan do its job. As soon as the light scanned over her eye, the door opened. Addie motioned the others to follow her, while Wolff stayed behind. Soon enough, the others were all inside and only he and Dusty were left.

"You go ahead man, I'll hold down the fort," Dusty offered.

"Not this time man, we can hold it down from inside," Wolff told him, giving him a little shove.

As Wolff turned to follow him in, he felt a cold grip on his right shoulder. The hold it had on him was aggressive and Wolff knew that someone wanted a fight. Fear quickly changed to anger and his instincts turned him around to face his attacker. As he whipped his body around, he felt the first ice cold punch to his mid-section. He was initially winded, but he came back fast. Wolff moved to the side as the dark shadow in front of him grabbed his arm, leaving several long deep scratches as Wolff pulled away. How could he fight something that wasn't flesh and blood?

"Wolff, this is your chance to finish what you started years ago," Isaac's voice said from behind him.

"Tell me how Isaac!" Wolff shouted. The mist surrounded him, taking his breath away. The weaker he got, the more the mist seemed to change from black to deep purple and finally to green.

"Release your anger Wolff, he's feeding on it," Isaac instructed.

Wolff realized that had been his problem on that fateful night in New Orleans. He'd gone after it in anger, which only fed it and made it stronger. Well, he'd be damned if he would make the same mistake twice. With the invisible claws still holding him, he forced himself to relax his muscles, as well as his mind. That's when he saw his unmistakable face. Wolff knew this man. He had killed this man. Looking into his face and remembering his sister's death, the anger started to swell up in him once again. As Wolff's anger grew, his grip grew stronger and the entity lifted Wolff off the ground. Then came the evil, unforgettable laugh he had heard once before.

"Concentrate Wolff! He will win unless you can take his energy from him," Isaac warned.

"Not this time Galan, and not ever again!" Wolff shouted. He forced himself to relax again, allowing his limbs to go limp. The grip on his arms loosened and Wolff dropped to the ground.

"Wolff, his name, call him by his given name and command him to leave. Fight with your words. If you don't, he'll kill you," Isaac called out.

"Not today," Wolff managed. "Galan Masterson? Not likely, more like Galan Masterson, puff of useless-smoke."

The mist seemed to pull back, forming a pillar directly in front of Wolff. This time, Wolff was ready. He took in a deep breath and filled his lungs. He felt Isaac directly behind him he was showing him pictures in his mind of how to fight with his words.

"Galan, I command you to be bound," Wolff was amazed and empowered to see what happened as he spoke the words Isaac instructed. As he spoke, what looked like a rope of white light surrounded the dark mist. The sound that emanated from the dark pillar was that of pain and anger. It twisted and turned to free itself as Wolff moved closer to the mass, commanding it to leave the property. It began to shrink and tried to lash out at him, throwing him backwards, but he didn't lose his footing. Holding his own, he continued to walk toward the mass, commanding it to leave in the name of our savior, Lord Jesus Christ. The closer he came to the mass, the thinner it became. There was a loud angry growl and a sucking sound, and it disappeared into the wall behind it.

Wolff held his stomach and turned to face Isaac.

"Good job on your first fight Wolff," Isaac said.

Wolff looked down at his arm that was bleeding from all the scratches. "A little training first would have been nice," Wolff countered.

"I would have stepped in, but you were doing fine. He's not only the hit man you knew Wolff, he was also Bright Star's student. The best way I can describe this encounter is similar to a bar fight. He'll be back and next time, he won't be alone. It's going to take all of us to fight this battle. Get inside and wrap that rib. It's not broken, but it's badly bruised and don't forget that those scratches were made by a dead, rotting soul. They will become infected if you don't take care of them immediately. Addie knows how to protect and train you. Pike and Angus will provide the rest of the weapons you'll need to practice."

"Isaac, first things first, Trask got any beer stashed in this cellar? You owe me a drink," Wolff said, holding his ribs. Wolff watched as the shadow of Isaac moved away from him, to one of the doors built into the wall of the tasting room.

"Here we are," Isaac said, stopping in front of one of the doors.

Wolff moved to open the door that turned out to be a refrigerator, stocked with several different brews.

"Now that's what I'm talking about," Wolff said. He toasted Isaac, downed the first one, and grabbed three more before heading for the door. "Snoop, you hear me?" Wolff asked.

"Always man, that was some fight, just wait until you see the play back," Snoop said.

"I'll settle for you opening the door," Countered Wolff.

"No problem, the boss can open it from the inside. I'll give her the all-clear," Snoop said.

"Not yet," Warned Isaac. "Wolff, put the beer down, we have to block them from entering this room."

Wolff downed the rest of his beer and followed Isaac back to the table.

"Grab the salt shaker there on the table. Take the lid off and follow me," Isaac instructed.

Wolff did as he was told. Isaac was leading him to the doorway of the tasting room.

"Put the salt all along the floor here in the doorway and repeat exactly what I say."

Wolff followed Isaac's instructions, closing off the entrance to the room as he straightened up, wincing from the pain in his ribs. Before Wolff could ask Isaac anything, he was gone.

Wolff sighed and walked back to the entrance of Trask's office, grabbing the remaining two beers from the table before he went. Just as he reached the door it opened, revealing Dusty. He was standing with his gun ready and was smiling ear to ear.

"You are the only one I know who can start a bar fight with a man, without actually being in a bar, and without involving an actual man, for that matter," Dusty said, jumping out of Wolff's way. He watched as Wolff quickly turned and stopped to pour the rest of the salt across the opening, while reciting the same words Isaac had taught him. Before Wolff headed down the hall, he instructed Dusty to secure the door, handing him one of the beers as he passed.

59

CHAPTER 9

Addie was waiting for him at the end of the hall. "You don't look too bad for a guy that just battled a...," started Addie.

"A what?" Wolff asked. "A dead man? A demon? Addie, what the hell did I just fight?" Before she could answer, he added. "Isaac said you should wrap my ribs and that you know how to treat these scratches. Damn things hurt like hell," Wolff said. He reached out to take a hold of Addie's arm before she went any further. "Addie, it was Galan. I saw his face, but I can't believe it. Isaac said he was Bright Star's student. I think it's time you tell me what you know about Galan and about me," Said Wolff. He didn't let Addie pull away as they continued into the conference area. Addie motioned for him to sit down so she could have a look at the scratches.

"What I know is that you are like me, maybe even stronger, we will have to see. As for Galan, he was supposed to be the second man on team W.I.S.E, but they backed off when they were unsuccessful with Bright Star."

"So, if Galan was to be second in command, who is Bright Star?" Wolff noticed the rest of the team gathering around them in the large conference area.

"There were rumors for years about the identity of Bright star, but no one except his handler knew for sure. The claim was that Bright Star had reached the sixth level."

"What happens at the sixth level?" Wolff asked.

"The sixth level of heaven contains the knowledge to heal and regenerate the body. It would be the best age-defying program out there, if only they could bottle it," Addie teased.

"One of the many gifts from God that we don't understand," Angus blurted out.

"Hey man, you want to see the instant replay?" The team heard Snoop ask.

"I do," Nick answered, and the rest of them smiled.

"Me too, kid," Wolff answered, wincing as Addie poured a thick yellow oily liquid on his scratches.

"Hey, watch it with that stuff, will ya?" Wolff said, pulling back.

"Don't be such a sissy."

"That's you alright, who else would let a puff of smoke throw him across the room like a rag doll," Ray said smiling.

"Puff of smoke? Yeah right, just a look at this," said Wolff, holding up his bleeding arm.

"So, you got a couple of scratches, big deal. Maybe if you talk nice, Ms. Holly might kiss it and make it all better. I have Intel from a very reliable source that says she's a great...," Bird started. As he stepped closer to Holly, she reached out to give him a shove.

"No need for that, I just wanted all you tough guys to know who saved your bacon, once again," said Wolff. He pulled off his shirt to let Addie wrap his ribs.

Wolff winced as she pulled the wrap tight.

"Go easy on him honey, he's had a rough day," Martin said. He handed Addie some bandages to finish dressing the scratches.

"Go ahead, laugh it up, all of you. Just wait until I learn how to deal with this thing. I plan on bringing new meaning to the phrase *things that go bump in the night*," Wolff said.

"As long as *it's* the one going bump, and not you," said Bat. "Holly, would you run that last part over again so Wolff can see himself on the big screen."

Wolff moved closer to stand right behind Holly. Leaning over, he whispered in her ear, "Let it roll baby."

"I'm not your baby," Holly answered, poking him with her elbow.

"Careful Ms. Holly, I'm an injured man," Wolff said, jumping back to avoid her jab to his ribs.

61

"You'll have to come up with a better line than that now that she's met some real men," Bird said.

"Real men?" Wolff asked, doubtfully looking around the room.

"Ms Holly, left several men eagerly anticipating her return to New Orleans," Dusty added.

"Is that so? I don't see any beads around her neck," Wolff said, looking over at Holly with raised eyebrows.

"That's because there were too many to wear, they made her neck hurt," Bird answered.

"You men are all full of it. Addie, you got any boots around here? It's starting to get deep," Bat said, looking over at Holly, shaking her head.

"We'll need hip waders if this keeps up. See what you started Holly? Can we please get down to business? Everyone, please be seated. Holly, would you bring up the video from the beginning? What I need to know is how many of you see more than just Wolff getting?" Addie started to ask.

"His hat handed to him?" Jacob asked.

"Yes, let's start with the color. Does anyone see a color surrounding Wolff?" Addie asked. No one raised their hand.

"You mean you guys can't see it?" Wolff asked.

"See what, man? All I see is you getting beat up by the invisible man," Dusty said.

"Holly, back it up just a little and then pause it," Holly did as she was asked and Wolff moved to the screen to point out an area directly in front of him. Now here, do you see this black and green mist?" Wolff asked. When he looked around the table, he saw everyone looking back at him with questioning looks. It was obvious that only Addie and Bat could see what he did.

"I see it Wolff, and I see his face," Addie said, "its Galan."

"I don't know who Galan is, but I see the color and his face," Bat added.

"I can't see his face, but I can assure you he's dead, I killed Galan myself," Jacob said.

"You're right Jacob, he's dead, but that just means he is out of his body. If the rumors are true about him achieving the sixth level of wisdom, then he survived longer and was more powerful than Bright Star," Addie told them.

"More powerful how?" Debbie asked.

"He made it without having his mind seared, like Bright Star, at least that's what we think happened," Addie answered.

"So, who do you think he killed before Jacob killed him?" Debbie asked.

"Angus, would you care to take this one?" Addie asked.

Angus stood to address the group. "We think the man Galan killed, was Bright Stars soul partners they call them. You see, just as in life, when we are out of the body we tend to, as the young ones say, hang with our homeboys," They all laughed. "What did I say?" No one responded they all just shook their heads. "As I was saying, when we are in the body we tend to look for those that we can associate with, such as bikers that ride together or those young people that wear all black."

"You mean the Goth look?" Holly asked.

"That's it. But when we are out of body, we don't see the way others look or move and we can't go by facial expressions, but what we can see is even more telling," Angus explained.

"I don't know, I can read a man pretty good. Good enough to win all of Wolff's money," Jacob said.

Angus smiled, "Son, as good as you may be at reading bodies, when you can see the color of the spirit it is almost fool proof."

"Almost?" Wolff asked.

"Yes, unfortunately they can appear as anything they want, to those who only look at the physical. However, for those who can see deeper, they can't hide their true colors," Angus said.

"I don't quite get it. If they can change into anything they want us to see, then how do we know that was Galan? Whatever it was might have just wanted us to think it was Galan," Jacob said.

"No, it was him, I know it was," Wolff said.

"Let's try this Mr. Wolff, if you disregard the face you saw, what else would make your think it was Galan? Shut your eyes if you need to," said Angus.

Wolff closed his eyes letting his mind go back the day he thought he'd killed Galan. What came to mind was the feeling he had, the feeling of an overwhelming power and the color green.

"Mr. Wolff, what do you remember? Don't leave anything out, every detail please, even if you think it's not important," Angus pushed.

"I remember an oppressive feeling around me. I could feel the air change around me and close in on me. Then the strangest thing, I kept seeing the color green. Like everything had a green tint to it. Then, as quick as it came, it was gone," Wolff told them.

"And that was the same feeling you had out there today?" Addie asked.

"Yeah, but the intensity was much stronger this time. What am I saying Addie? I don't believe in any of this," Wolff told her.

"First of all, you don't have to believe it and second, he is stronger now that his body is not holding him back. He and Bright Star are both out of body now," Addie told him.

"She's right, he's stronger now without the body, but there are still rules he's bound by and believe it or not, you're still stronger," Angus explained.

"So how do we back up our man if none of us can see this thing?" Dusty asked.

64

"You don't, I do," Addie said, "What you can do is keep it a clean fight by keeping the rest of his cohorts out of the way."

"But if we can't see them, how do we keep them out of the way?" Bird asked.

"The ones you'll be able to help with are still in the body and they're the ones calling the shots," Addie explained. "The plan is to shut down the bosses and then bind the others."

"So where do we start?" Bird asked.

"We start with Wolff getting trained and the rest of you tracking down the bosses," Addie answered.

"What do we do when we find them?" Ray asked.

"We eliminate them," Pike answered, looking over at Addie who nodded in approval.

"Where we go from there remains to be seen," Addie said.

"What my wife is trying to say is, one step at a time," said Martin.

"Well put," Angus said.

"By now I'm sure the bosses know where to find us or at least know we're in Panama, so we need to make the next strike," Addie told them. "Ray, while Angus, Debbie and I are working with Wolff, you're in charge,"

"Divide and concur Boss? Works for me," Ray answered.

"Be careful up top, we have no idea how or when they will attack," said Addie.

"As long as we're here, there are all kinds of safe guards, including bullet and explosive proof glass in all the windows," Jacob explained. "Ray, I know all the tricks of this place. I'll help Holly and Snoop get the info loaded up if they don't have it."

"Good, let's get started. Wolff, Angus, Debbie, and I will meet you all back up top for dinner. Pike, you're cooking," Addie instructed. Jacob nodded to Ray, while Pike smiled at Addie. At least for now he had a job he liked. They watched as the others left with Ray in the lead and Dusty bringing up the back.

"Take good care of them Ray," Addie called out.

"I'll take good care of Ms. Holly," Ray called back. Dusty tipped his cowboy hat at Wolff and winked.

"Just take care of yourself man," Wolff called out. Addie could hear the anger in his voice.

"Go learn how to fight smoke, Wolff man, and leave the flesh and blood ladies to the real men," Ray called back.

"Addie, he's mine when this is done. I know you like him, but you can always find a new pit bull," Wolff said. "Let's get this thing over with, where do we start?" Wolff asked all business.

"We start in the black room, in the dark," Addie answered smiling.

CHAPTER 10

Ray stopped the group at the elevator doors. "Snoop, what's the status up top?"

"All clear Ray, reflectors are up so you can see out, but no one can see in. Pike, you're going to love the kitchen," Snoop answered.

"You forget Snoop, I've been here before. What I can't wait to see is Wolff in the kitchen," Pike answered and everyone turned to stare at him. "Addie is hard pressed to know who the best chef is, and she wants a cook-off between myself, Tan and Wolff, when this is over."

"Hey, wait a minute I want some of that action. I'm really good in the kitchen, right Martin?" Nick said.

"Right you are partner. He may give you Chef's a run for your money," Martin answered.

Ray hit the button on the elevator with a closed fist. "I got a feeling this is going to be an interesting case," He said, smiling over at Holly.

"I think you're right Boss," Holly answered.

When the elevator doors opened, no one moved. At first sight, the hallway was like walking into a museum. Holly followed Ray out, walking past him to the wall opposite the elevator doors, staring at the vase sitting atop an ornate table.

"My God, this is a pot from the Ming dynasty and this table is…"

"It's a Louis the 14th? Follow me people," Ray said. Taking Holly by the elbow he guided her on. "Pull up the floor plan and locate a good place to set up command. There should be a conference room or something close to the center of this floor."

"There is, straight ahead. Here take a left, come on. There is a right up here and one more left, just look at this art work…," Holly said as she moved.

"Mr. Trask sure did like paintings and vases," Nick said.

"Oh, that's nothing young man, wait until you see the game room," Pike told him.

"Here it is, the conference room should be right behind these doors," said Holly, "that is a room big enough to accommodate us."

"I remember this room. You're right Holly, it's big enough to accommodate us, but it's not your ordinary conference room," Pike said.

"Jacob, can you get us in?" asked Ray.

"Nope, I'm not on record for this room," Jacob answered.

"I am," Pike said. He moved quickly to take hold of the massive handles in the center of each one of the huge mahogany doors. As he did, the handles glowed and he pulled the doors back. Martin held one as Ray grabbed the other. Pike walked through the doors with the others following close behind, every eye was scanning the room.

"Welcome to Trask's Library," Pike said. He stood in the middle of the huge oval room, waving his hands as he turned, like a circus ring master pointing out acts.

"Holly, Martin and Nick, set up the computers and screens over there on the first two tables. It would help if you moved them together. Pike, you and Dusty move the lamps off the tables and put them somewhere safe, so we have some room to set up. I'm going to check in with Addie. Bird, you and Bat see if you can find some more chairs," Ray said. He pulled out his phone as the others went to work, with Holly directing.

"Boss, phase one is underway, we're setting up the war room in the library. As soon as we have it all set up, I'll let Snoop brief everyone on phase two and then we'll disperse to the local office. Any idea what you want us to look for or should we just get what we can?" Ray asked.

"We need full recon of the offices. It may take you a couple of days and we need to be sure no one knows we're there. No one can see anyone go in or out we need to keep our identities concealed as long as possible. The longer we can keep them guessing as to who and how many team members are here, the faster we can tie this thing up," Addie told him.

"You got it Boss. I'll be in touch," Ray answered and signed off. When he turned around to face the group, everyone was around the table. Holly, with her pad, was bringing up the computer.

"We're ready when you are," she said.

"I could get used to this girl. Patch in Snoop and bring up the virtual of the Panama office and the surrounding area. Let's do a four-to-eight block radius," said Ray.

"Snoop, here, you're in the driver's seat. Ray, Where to?"

"Show me the cameras live feed inside the office. Holly, I need a split screen; building plans on one side and Snoop's live feed from the cameras on the other," Ray instructed.

"As you can see, the office is in a secluded area. There is a way in and out from every angle of the building. If all else fails, we can enter and live via the connected tunnels under the street, they go out on either side to the shops next to the office. The other one goes across the street and comes up in the coffee shop. From the back of the coffee shop, you can enter the shops on either side," Snoop explained.

"How'd we get so lucky? Trask make some kind of deal with them?" Ray asked.

"Nope, he just bought the block and handpicked the people to run the shops."

"You mean to tell me the business owners are ex...," Ray started to ask.

"Everyone for two blocks, that being said, I've made arrangements for you all to catch rides in. Bird, you and Bat will split up. Bird, I have a motorcycle on the lower level waiting for you. Take it to the men's clothing shop next to the office and go in from there. Bat, you'll be dropped off by one of our local food suppliers at the bus stop. Take a bus ride to the café across from the office. To make it look good, take a table outside and order a cup of coffee until I tell you to go in. Ray, you and Holly will be picked up here by the bakery truck that used to deliver milk and baked goods here to Trask. They will take the two of you into the Bakery and you can enter the office from there," Snoop instructed.

"Hey, how come Ray gets to ride in the bakery truck?" Nick asked.

"Because we have to pay for everything we eat and Ray hates sweets," Snoop retorted. "Now, that brings me to Nick, Martin and Jacob. Jacob, you and Martin will have to dress up for this one. The two of you are going in as art dealers to the gallery on the other side of the office."

"We can handle dressing up, right Martin?" Jacob asked.

"Yeah, but how do we handle all the attention from the ladies?" Martin said.

"Yeah, because every girl is crazy about a sharp dressed man, right?" Holly added, watching all the men smile while shaking their heads.

"You got that right. I like this lady more every minute you looking for a good man Ms. Holly?" Jacob asked.

"Careful Jacob, you'll have a Wolff tracking you," Ray said.

"Thank you Jacob, but I'm not looking for a man right now. As for Wolff, he can howl all he wants, but I am not anyone's one-night stand," Holly told them.

"A woman that knows her own mind, with some fire too, no wonder Wolff's interested. See dear, the problem with men in our line of work is that we need women that are also employed or at least trained like we've been. This is necessary so that the running and dodging life is something that they can live with. That makes you a prime asset, so to speak," Jacob answered.

"Prime asset? She's not a car Jacob," Dusty said.

"Guys, as much as I love discussing Ms. Holly's attributes, we have a job to do. Now, can I finish please?" Snoop asked sarcastically.

Nick, you're going in with Jacob and Martin, but you're going to have a little rougher ride I'm afraid," Snoop warned.

"I can take it; how will I go in?" Nick asked, puffing out his chest.

"You'll be in the crate that Jacob and Martin will be delivering to the art gallery," explained Snoop.

"Wait a minute; did you say you're going to stuff me in a crate?" Nick asked.

"I thought you said you had what it takes to run with the big dogs?" Ray countered.

"I can, but a crate?"

"Would you rather dress up and wear a tie?" Martin asked.

"And maybe a straw hat?" Jacob added.

"I'll take the crate," answered Nick.

"Nick, I once had to hide under some seats in a boat. It was like a coffin and smelled like one too, but we have do what the plan calls for. I'm not wild about riding on busses either," Bat said, patting him on the shoulder.

"And, you'll be less wild about the sun dress I picked out for you to wear, I'm sure," said Snoop. "Dusty, you'll be following Jacob and Martin in the black panel truck with Nick in the back. You will all go in. Dusty will unload the crate and you'll enter the office from the art gallery. Does anyone have any questions?"

"You want me to wear a sun dress?" Bat asked.

"And a big brimmed hat. I want you to blend in sweetheart and I thought the combat gear would draw attention," Snoop answered.

71

"She's gonna draw attention when she shows those legs of hers," Bird said.

"Snoop, if you've got one of those big skirt wrap-around things, or any kind of lacy frock, I just want you to know you're a dead man. I will hunt you down and...," Bat said.

"Hey Bat, you gotta do what the plan calls for," Nick said, looking over at her.

"This kid learns fast," Jacob said and laughed as Bat reached out and gave Nick's shoulder a shove.

"Don't worry Bat, I let my wife pick out the dress for you and the boys will love it. I don't think they will even notice your legs," Snoop added.

"I want to hear that from Kore herself," Bat demanded.

"Hey Bat, I thought you might want to be reassured. I did pick it out for you. It's a basic sundress, yellow and orange, with poppy red flowers. It is fitted in all the right places, the straps meet and button behind the neck, giving you a perfect V neckline. The skirt is fitted at the waist and flows nicely, flaring slightly around the bottom. I think you'll love the hat and accessories I picked out," Kore told her.

"I don't know, but that sounds a lot better than my crate," Nick said to Bat and ducked before she could shove him again.

"Thanks Kore, you saved your man's life," Bat said smiling.

"Yeah, don't worry Bat, I still pick out or design the entire undercover wardrobe for the ladies in this group. If I let Snoop do it and he sent you ladies out, well let's just say you might look professional, but not the right kind," Kore said.

"Hey, I don't...," Snoop started to say, but Kore stopped him mid-sentence.

"He agrees, don't you dear?" Kore asked.

"Yes dear, I do," answered Snoop.

"Oh brother," Nick added.

"On with business, Holly, Snoop will guide you through the house to everyone's quarters. Everything we just talked about is waiting for each of you. Holly, when you're done meet me in the kitchen. The bakery truck should be here in about an hour or so, right Snoop?" Ray asked. "That's right, lead on Holly," answered Snoop.

CHAPTER 11

"One team is in place, what do you guys say we get started?" Addie said, looking around at Debbie, Angus and Wolff.

"Lead the way Boss, I got your back," Wolff answered.

Addie nodded and headed out of the cellar to the elevator. Once in, she pushed three and looked over at her three team members and said, "Let the adventure begin."

"We're not going all the way to the top, are we?" Wolff asked.

"How many floors are there?" Debbie asked.

"Floor five is the main house, as we called it. Floor three is where Trask conducted his ongoing work on what he called the Solomon Project. Wolff, you and Debbie are some of the few people to see this floor. Trask and Isaac of course used this area. The only other ones to see it were...," Addie answered.

"Myself, my brother Marcus, Jacob and Pike, correct me if I'm wrong Addie?" Angus asked.

"You're never wrong, at least that's what you always tell me, Angus," Addie added. She loved to watch Angus's tummy bounce when he chuckled.

"So why you Angus?" Debbie asked.

"Because they know the most about King Solomon's activities, right?" Addie asked.

"Each player has a part. Addie, you are correct, both Pike and I do know a great deal about Solomon and his activities, but Pike's degrees in Quantum Physics helped. My brother Marcus is our prayer cover and metaphysical trainer. Addie was their student and Jacob...," Angus explained.

"Jacob was the hired gun," Wolff said. He didn't turn around to look at anyone as the doors to the elevator opened on the third floor.

"Right you are young man," Angus said, passing Wolff as they all filed out into the hallway. Wolff was bringing up the rear.

Before them was another door that looked extremely heavy, along with several scanners on the side wall. Addie walked over and punched in a code on the keypad. A green light lit up a hand pad that flipped out of the wall toward her. She laid her hand on the pad, making sure her finger tips touched the rims of the imprint, and then she pressed down hard. They all watched as the light from the scanner went back and forth a couple of times, and then shown bright green as the wall seemed to suck the pad back into it. Addie leaned forward for the last scan, placing her eyes close to a small light on the door, allowing it to verify her retina. When the low beep sounded, she stepped back as the huge door swung open.

"Hurry through everyone, it will only be open for twenty seconds," Addie said.

Wolff had just crossed the threshold as the door swung shut and a loud locking sound could be heard from somewhere inside the massive thing.

"It reminds me of a bank vault," said Debbie.

"Trask once told me the toymakers gathered information from the best designers, and then three of them split up the design of the door. They did this so that no one person would know the entire design," Addie explained.

"The more I learn about the team you have at Solomon, the more I have to wonder how you keep the security so tight. I mean, if someone left, how could you ever trust that they wouldn't leak information?" Debbie asked.

The rest of the team looked around at each other and smiled.

"That's simple, no one has ever left. Some members of our team have died, but no one that is still living has ever left Solomon Inc.," Addie answered.

"But someone could, aren't you afraid someone could get a hold of me and I could spill something?" Debbie asked.

"No, because if they did, we would shoot you," Wolff said.

"Wolff, stop that. We would not shoot anyone. To answer your question Debbie, everyone who wants to know more about Solomon already knows that anyone we bring in will know nothing of value. They would have to have one of the partners in order to get any helpful information. Second of all, the men and women we have working for us, well let's just say that they are no longer loved by their previous employers. Solomon provides a safe haven for those who have certain talents, but nowhere to go. And we also pay very well," Addie explained, giving Wolff a dirty look.

"You mean they're all mercenaries?" Debbie asked.

"I prefer Soldier for Fortune," Wolff replied. Debbie smiled back at him.

"Just one more question," said Debbie.

"Sure, we have time for one more," Addie answered.

"If the partners are the ones that knew the whole story and you're the only partner left, but you don't know all of the information, how are we ever going to find out? Is some information is lost?" Debbie asked.

"Brilliant question dear," Angus said, "first, we're going to enter the data storage banks."

"How are we going to get into them? Addie, do you have the codes?" Debbie asked, following after Angus.

Angus stopped short, Debbie almost ran into him. "No, Addie doesn't have the codes and she doesn't know how to put the puzzle pieces together, none of us do."

"Then how are we going to do anything?" Debbie asked.

"We're here to ask the men who do know," answered Addie.

"Precisely, and you're going to help us," Angus told her. Taking hold of the door knob, he pushed the door open,

76

reached in to turn on a light and stood back to allow the ladies to pass.

Debbie followed Addie, and was now more confused than ever.

"I love it when a plan comes together," Wolff said. After guiding Angus through the door, Wolff followed closely and shut the door tight behind them.

The room was not what either Debbie or Wolff expected. The room's entire left side was completely black. Portable computer desks and chairs were scattered throughout the room. There were also some kind of control panels with a wide array of buttons and levers. At the end stood tall shelves with strange looking helmets, in the center of the room stood two chairs next to each other. The chairs reminded Wolff of dentist chairs.

"I don't need any dental work done," Wolff said.

"Don't worry, it's not your teeth we're after," Addie said. Crossing the room, she grabbed two helmets from the shelf and handed one to Wolff.

"Then what are you after?" Wolff asked, taking the helmet from her.

"We want your mind, soul and spirit all working together," said Angus. Offering Debbie his arm, he led her to the side of the room back behind the equipment and pulled a chair up for her behind one of the control panels.

"Wait a minute, you want my what?" Wolff demanded.

"What's the matter, is the big tough Wolff scared?" Addie asked.

"Damn straight, you take me into a dark room with creepy looking dentist chairs and..."

"You don't see a drill, do you?" Angus asked.

"No, but I see restraints and this thing you want me to put on my head."

"Don't you trust me Wolff? Then again, I guess it does seem strange for a woman to be after your mind instead of your," said Addie. As she walked to stand beside one of the chairs, she patted the arm rest and smiled back at him.

"Very funny, never mind what the women in my life are after. Let's get on with this thing," Addie looked back at Angus and Debbie, who both nodded with approval.

"Which chair Angus?" Addie asked.

"You mean I have to sit in a certain chair? What's the difference?"

"Yes, the proper chair is important to the flow of energy between the entities. The difference is the color. Mr. Wolff, please take the blue one, Addie will strap you in. Addie, you take the red next to Mr. Wolff and I will strap you in," Angus instructed.

"Seriously? Energy flow, strapped in, none of this is making me feel any better Angus."

"Sit down. You can let the helmet sit on your lap," said Addie, sounding a little more annoyed than she meant to. Wolff did as he was told and took a seat. Addie set the helmet down gently on his lap and started to apply the restraints at his wrists first, and then moved to his ankles.

"Watch it Addie, you're married and this could put me in the mood," Wolff teased.

"The wind blowing puts you in the mood, as I recall," Addie shot back.

"So why the restraints anyway?" Wolff asked. Before Addie could answer they heard Angus voice come across the speakers.

"I'll take it from here Addie," Angus said. Addie smiled at Wolff and walked to her chair, where Angus was waiting to put on her restraints.

"Ready on the platform, Miss Debbie, would you please turn the black dial in front of you to four?" Angus asked.

Debbie nodded back and slowly turned the dial to four. Suddenly, she noticed a soft blue spot light appearing above the platform.

"Is this acceptable to you Addie, or would you prefer another color?" Angus asked softly.

"Being that this is Wolff's first time, can you take it up a little to lavender?" Addie asked.

"Addie, you know better than that, this is far from my first time," Wolff said and winked at her.

"It will be your first time at this destination," Addie answered and winked back.

"Miss Debbie, please continue to turn the dial to four and a half, if you would."

Again, Debbie turned the dial and watched the light above them.

"Are we ready?" Angus asked.

"We are. Wolff, from now on you will hear Angus walking you through the steps to come to what the founders called the round table. See you in the middle," Addie answered as Angus slid the helmet down over her head, adjusting the straps as he talked softly to Addie. When he'd finished with the helmet he adjusted her chair back so she could recline.

"No snoring Addie," Wolff said, as Angus turned to assist him.

"She can't hear you Mr. Wolff, you'll see once you are wearing your helmet," Angus explained as he picked Wolff's helmet up off his lap.

"Explain this thing before you put it on my head. Why can't Addie hear anything?" Wolff said gruffly.

"I will explain as I go. For you it will not be total deprivation, you will hear my instructions. This helmet and this room serve as a large deprivation chamber. I'm sure you're familiar with the use of them, as an operative you would have had some training," said Angus.

"I am, but I've seen worse in Afghanistan, only there they called them black holes," Wolff answered.

"How did you do?" Angus asked.

"I slept most of the way through it, that is when they weren't torturing me or trying to...," Wolff answered.

"How did you get out?" Angus asked.

"I over-powered one of the guards when he came to take me for another torture session. Then, I killed everyone in sight with his weapons, then hotwired one their trucks and headed out. That's when I contacted Addie. See, the founders were trying to hire me for their team, but I wanted to stay in the military," said Wolff.

"What made you change your mind, was it the money?" Angus asked.

"Nope, the betrayal of Uncle Sam when I made contact to tell them I had escaped. They told me, in so many words, that my services were no longer needed and no one was coming to extract me. I wasn't worth it to them. I guess that was the plan all along, they just never thought I'd complete the mission and live to tell about it," Wolff said. "They were so sure I wouldn't make it out, they didn't even bother to ask me if I had obtained the object they sent me to retrieve."

"That's awful, the fact that our Government does...," Debbie said from across the room.

"Happens every day Miss Debbie. Just like the Devil, when Uncle Sam is done with you, he has no problem killing his own.

So, what happened next?" Debbie asked.

"Addie had given me a contact number, so I found a land line and called her. The rest is history, as they say. The founders sent Addie, Ray and Jacob to extract me. As soon as we were out I was examined and allowed to rest up. Once I felt up to it, I told Isaac I would be back when I had finished hunting," Wolff answered.

"So, you took some time to go to the woods and do some hunting? Well that sounds nice," Debbie said. Both men looked at each other and smiled. "What?" Debbie asked.

80

"Miss Debbie, I didn't go to the woods to hunt animals, I went straight to the black forest of Washington and killed everyone who'd left me in that hellhole."

"Didn't they come after you?" Debbie asked.

"It took them too long to figure out who did it. By that time, I was a member of Solomon. Why they didn't come after me always baffled me, that's one question I'm going to ask the founders," Wolff told her.

"So, they just forgot about it and let you go?" Debbie pressed.

"Not exactly, they killed my sister, to try and draw me out," Wolff told her. Both men could hear the sharp intake of air from Debbie.

"I am so sorry Mr. Wolff, I had no idea. I would have never pressed...," Debbie said.

"Miss Debbie, no worries. I went after the man who did it and killed him, or at least I thought I had. Now I find out he lived for years in a comma and it turns out that he was Bright Star in training. So, teach me what I need to know Angus, because next time he comes for me, ghost or not, I can send him to hell where he belongs," Wolff said, looking Angus square in the eye.

"In order to talk to the others, Mr. Wolff, you'll have to cross over," Angus said.

"Then put that damn thing on my head and let's get on with it," Wolff answered.

Angus smiled as he lowered the helmet over Wolff's head. Wolff couldn't believe how it shut everything out. No light, no sound, everything was pitch black. Wolff's fist sensation was a rush of panic, but he forced himself to breath deep and lay back, consciously relaxing his muscles. It was as though time stood still.

"What's next Angus? Hey man you out there?" Wolff asked. That's when he heard Angus's voice at his ear, through the helmet.

"I am Mr. Wolff I'm going to walk you through the door so that you can take your place at the table. Are you ready?"

"Ready as I'll ever be," Wolff answered, relaxing down into the chair.

"Mr. Wolff, relax completely. I want you to feel your muscles, each group one at a time, become like lead. I want you to see the door before you. Let go in your mind and see the door open. Tell me, Mr. Wolff, who do you see on the other side?" Angus asked.

Wolff took a deep breath. *This was ridiculous,* he thought, but then he saw the door. Angus must be projecting a door with this helmet. He'd fix this *I can't see a door if my eyes are shut,* Wolff thought, but the door was still there.

"Shutting your eyes won't make us go away," Wolff heard Addie say. With his eyes shut, Wolff could still see the door and Addie standing across the threshold. However, her voice was not coming from the helmet. With his eyes still closed, he saw himself standing and walking toward the door.

"We're waiting Wolff," He heard Isaac's voice from the other side of the door.

Wolff walked straight to the door, *if Addie could do this so could he.* As he crossed the threshold, he felt the warm sensation of water cascade over him, just as Bat had always described it. Then he was through, standing on the other side. Again, he felt panic starting. This time Addie stepped forward to take his hand. The minute she touched him, every muscle relaxed and he felt a peace like he'd never known. What he saw, he would later come to know as the board room. There was a round table in the middle, and the rest of the room remained hidden in the shadows. Seated at the table were both Isaac and Trask, looking younger than him.

"Please, be seated Mr. Wolff," Trask said, motioning him to one of the empty chairs.

Wolff followed Addie to the table, pulled out a chair for her and took the empty chair next to hers. Wolff noticed that there were two empty chairs at the table. Debbie watched as Angus turned on one screen after another, revealing brightly colored charts.

"Angus, what is all this? Why did you stop talking to Wolff?" Debbie asked.

"Addie's with him. He's crossed over and these are monitoring what's going on in the meeting. We can use this for future training. It also helps me keep track of Addie and Mr. Wolff's vital signs," Angus explained.

"What do you mean we can see what's going on in the meeting?" Debbie asked.

"Look at this monitor," Angus said, turning on the big screen TV monitor behind them on the wall. As Debbie watched in amazement, what she saw was four people sitting around a round table talking. There was no sound, but she could see them so clearly, it was as though she was in the room with them.

"How are we seeing this and why is there no sound?" Debbie asked.

"Addie is projecting back to me what she is seeing. There is no sound because they are in a deprived mode within the helmets. Her mind is projecting this back, but we'll have to wait to find out what they are talking about until the computer has a chance to read their lips and add in the words. It will all be recorded for future reference," Angus explained.

"Angus, how did they get in that room? How are both of them seeing the same thing, they're just sitting in those chairs and they aren't even moving," said Debbie. Angus could hear both curiosity and fear in her voice.

"Their bodies are here in the chairs, but their spirits are, what Addie calls, in-between," Angus explained.

"So, what do we do?" Debbie asked.

"We watch and pray Ms. Debbie; will you join me?" Angus asked. Reaching for her hand, they walked over to the plush easy chairs that sat opposite the monitors. From the coffee table, he picked up a Bible and handed it to Debbie. "Can I get you something to drink before we start?"

"Water please," Debbie said.

"A wedge of lemon?" Angus asked.

"You have lemons down here?"

"If the servants have had a chance to do their jobs we will. Yes, here it is," Angus said. He took two glasses from the shelf above the small bar and reached down to open the small fridge beneath the bar. He set a small bowl of lemon wedges and a large bottle of imported water on the bar. Debbie watched as he opened the bottle of cold water, pouring it into the two glasses over the wedges of lemon. Then, he returned the lemon and the bottle of water to the fridge, picked up the glasses and crossed the room back to where Debbie was sitting. Angus handed Debbie her glass.

"What did you mean doing their job?" Debbie asked, accepting the glass.

"The servants that cook and clean, among other things, are here every day following Trask's instructions," Angus answered, taking a drink of his water. "Ahh lemon, do you know almost every culture who has access to lemons uses them for cleansing the body inside and out?"

"That's nice to know, but why would the servants continue to keep up the house now that Mr. Trask is dead? Who's paying for all this?" Debbie asked, waving her hand in the air. Angus chuckled before he answered.

"I keep forgetting you aren't familiar with how Solomon works. I guess it's time for a Bible lesson. Do you remember how King Solomon received the wisdom of God?" Angus asked.

"I do," Debbie answered, opening up the Bible to second Chronicles to read. "That night God appeared to

Solomon and said ask for anything you want me to give you."

When she looked over at Angus, she saw the water glass pressed to his lower lip and a broad smile across his face.

"Very good Ms. Debbie, please keep reading until I tell you to stop," Angus answered, looking straight ahead.

Debbie took another drink of water then continued. "Solomon answered God by saying 'you have shown great kindness to David, my father, and have made me king in his place. Now, Lord God, let your promise to my father David be confirmed for you have made me king over a people who are as numerous as the dust of the earth. Give me wisdom and knowledge, that I may lead this people, for who is able to govern this great people of yours?'"

"God said to Solomon, 'since this is your heart's desire and you have not asked for wealth, riches, or honor, nor the death of your enemies and since you've have not asked for a long life but for wisdom and knowledge to govern my people over whom I have made you king, therefore, wisdom and knowledge will be given you. And I will also give you wealth, riches, and honor, such as no king who was before you ever had and none after you will have."

"That's enough dear. That's where it all began, with one man's request of wisdom and God's covenant to one of his chosen ones. To grant it to him and him alone, is that how you read it Miss Debbie?" Angus asked.

"Yes, it says to him and no other. So, how did all this happen? How could anyone connected with Solomon Inc. or whatever branch of the government we're dealing with hope to obtain the Wisdom of Solomon that was between him and God?"

"Ah yes, it was between Solomon and God, that is until his servant Solomon wrote it down," Angus replied.

"Wrote it down or not, it was God's covenant with Solomon, he doesn't have to bless or cooperate with anyone else that uses it," Debbie said.

"That is true, except for a couple of key factors. First, let us examine one of the natures of God the father. When he gives, he gives freely and in abundance praise his name, correct Miss. Debbie?" Angus asked.

"If I recall correctly, pressed down and overflowing," Debbie answered.

"As I've heard it said in some of the churches I've attended, praise the Lord, preach it forward Sister," Angus said seriously.

Debbie couldn't help but laugh, it just seemed so strange coming from him.

"What is it? Did I get it wrong?" He asked.

"No, it just doesn't seem to fit coming from you. I mean, with your brother being a Bishop in the Catholic Church and all. Does he know you're visiting protestant churches? Wouldn't he be upset?" Debbie asked.

"It's also written that my brother is not my keeper, dear lady. I enjoy my visits to the services they are so full of life and happiness," He told her.

"And your brother's services aren't?" Debbie asked.

"We're getting off the subject Ms. Debbie, so let's just say my brother's services are somewhat more reserved."

"You mean stuffy?"

"Good word my lady. Now, back to our King Solomon, as we just established when God gives he can't help himself, he gives his all and that's what he did for the King."

"So, what are you saying?"

"Don't you see Ms. Debbie, if God is to give his full wisdom to Solomon, it would include the wisdom of evil, and the part it plays in God's plan and how to control it or should I say how to use it."

"I'm afraid I still don't understand."

"Don't worry, store this little bit away in your heart and it will make more sense as time goes on. As for your original question about the servants, Trask handpicked them and trained them how to maintain the compound. He made provision through the small bank near the main office for them to be paid like clockwork every week. He was very clear in his instructions that they were to continue with their work regardless of his being here or not. Trask even left instructions on how to pass on the care of the compound to their children," Angus explained.

"I have to admit Angus, the more I know about Solomon Inc. the stranger things get," said Debbie. She was finished with her water and set the glass down.

"Ms. Debbie, as the old saying goes, you ain't seen nothing yet," said Angus. Before he could continue, the computer began to relay the conversation of the meeting. Debbie looked over at the screen and listened to the mechanical voice. "Splendid, the programs caught up we can hear their discussion, let me turn it up."

CHAPTER 12

"You guys look like clowns. I'm sure glad I can wear jeans and a t-shirt," Nick said, pointing at Jacob and Martin.

"Yeah, but I'll be outside with the ladies while your little jean covered behind will be curled up in a box," Jacob answered, pulling on the lapels of his suite coat.

"I already got all the women I need in my life, I got a mom and a girlfriend," Nick told him, puffing out his chest.

"Yeah, what's your girlfriend's name? You think she's gonna wait for you now that you left her all alone?" Jacob asked, smiling over at Martin.

"Her name is Lilly, she's a real hottie and she loves me so much she'd wait forever. I'll always be able to find her."

"That's only because your mom is going to marry her dad," Martin added.

"You're dating your sister? Man, we need to talk," answered Jacob.

"She's not my real sister...," Nick started to say when Holly walked in the room.

"Wait, you mean I've been thrown over for a younger woman?" asked Holly. She walked into the room dressed in a coral colored flowered sundress.

"You're dating two women at the same time? Does Addie know this? Man that's wrong, right Martin," Jacob asked. He was trying very hard not to laugh out loud, while Martin covered his face with his hands in an effort to hold back the laughter.

"Don't worry Miss Holly, I'm sure you'll find someone else closer to your own age," said Nick.

"I'm heartbroken Nick, and that's the best you can do?" Holly demanded.

"I'm pretty good at mending broken hearts sweetheart," Jacob said. He moved close to Holly and slid his arm around her, pulling her close.

"You're going to have to start taking applications," Martin told her.

"I'll get mine in first, she's riding with me," Ray said, pushing Jacob's hand off Holly's waist.

"No problem Ray-man, I bow to the boss," Jacob answered.

"If you boys are done harassing Miss Holly, can we get this show on the road?" They heard Bat say from the doorway.

"Wow girl, Bird was right, you clean up good. Are you sure you don't want to trade up?" Jacob asked.

"I just might, you boys sure look sharp," said Bat, walking over to stand between Jacob and Martin.

"Now you're talking," Jacob said, offering her his elbow to hold.

"Yes, it's just too bad Addie beat me to you Martin," Bat said smiling back at Jacob, pretending she didn't notice his arm.

"That's cold baby," Jacob answered, lowering his arm.

"I hope that suit helps you out with the ladies in town, since it's not working so good for you here," Nick said.

"Watch it kid, you need me to get you out of the crate," Jacob reminded him as they followed Bat to the garage.

In the garage, they found their rides. The Baker was waiting with a coat for Ray. He pointed to the passenger seat. Ray climbed in as the Baker escorted Holly to a comfortable seat in the back. Seeing Nick's mouth water, he let him pick out a couple of pastries for the trip. The food vendor handed Bat a straw hat as she slid in the front seat. The cargo van driver, along with Jacob and Martin, secured Nick inside a crate, which had a folding chair for him to sit and ample ventilation. Before they closed the side, Nick put his hand up.

"So, where's your ride?" Nick asked Martin and Jacob.

"Under the tarp over there," Jacob said. He walked over to remove the tarp cover and revealed a brand-new Porsche 918 Spyder silver convertible.

"Is that your car Jacob?" Bat asked.

"I wish, and baby just saying, you'd look better in it than Martin. Sorry Martin," Jacob answered.

"Hey, I think so too," Martin agreed.

"Wow...," was all Nick could say as he jumped down and ran over to the car for a closer look. "You guys get to ride in this and I have to ride in a crate?"

"Nick when this is all over, with Addie's permission of course, I'll give you your first driving lesson. Will that be all right with you?" Asked Jacob.

"Martin, you won't tell my mom or Lilly, will you?" Nick asked.

"Not on your life, I'm already going to have to answer to those two when I get back just for letting you come along."

"Move out everyone," Ray called.

"You want to drive?" Jacob asked Martin.

"Glad you asked I never fight with a man who can shoot me from over a mile away," Martin said. He climbed in and fired it up, while Jacob checked behind the passenger seat. Martin heard him say "yes" as he pulled two hand guns out from behind the seat before getting in. He looked over at Martin.

"No problem man, it's easier for me to shoot if I'm not driving. Got your ear bud in?"

"Anticipating trouble?" Martin asked. He adjusted his ear bud by tapping it on, while waiting for Jacob's orders.

"Always anticipate the worst and have a plan B whenever you can," Jacob answered, buckling himself in.

"Welcome boys, your GPS is all set up. How'd I do on the fire arms?" Snoop asked.

"Not bad, I'll let Martin take the Wilson Beretta and I'll take the Special Forces Glocks. You got more ammo hidden around this tuna can?" Jacob asked as he turned on the GPS and motioned for Martin to head out of the compound.

"All over it, do you remember my usual places?" Snoop asked.

"Yeah, I do," Jacob answered, bending forward to reach under the seat.

"So, Jacob, if we are a rich guy art collector that drives a million-dollar sports car, do you think we would drive fast?" Martin asked.

"Sure, why else would you have a car like this?"

"I was just wondering when you were going to buckle up," Martin said. Before Jacob could answer, Martin shifted into first gear and hit the gas. Jacob grabbed for the dash with one hand and the seat belt with the other as Martin, following the GPS instructions, rounded a sharp curve with ease.

"Damn man, you've been holding out on us," Jacob said, rushing to buckle his seat belt.

"What?" Martin said, speeding along the road.

"What? Where did you learn to drive like this man?"

"I've been driving all my life. I'm a bad boy, just like the rest of you, I just grew up a few years back when I met Addie and really settled down," Martin told him.

"Well do me a favor Martin, stay bad while you're on this job, we need all the help we can get. What's our ETA?" Jacob asked.

"Hell if I know, I can't understand this thing, I just turn when it says turn," Martin answered. Jacob leaned forward, pressed a button on the built-in GPS and made his request.

"ETA?" Jacob asked. To his and Martin's surprise a very sexy sounding woman's voice, unlike the GPS directional voice, answered. "Your expected time of arrival is thirty minutes from now given your current rate of speed. Would you like me to update you should conditions change?"

"Baby you can update me anytime," Jacob answered. Martin laughed and took the next turn as directed.

"Jacob, can I ask you something?"

"You can ask, but I can't promise I'll answer."

"How did you get into this? I mean working for Solomon. Were you part of the original government project?" Martin asked.

"I wasn't part of the original project. I was a sniper that Trask hired for a job and that's when my life changed. Next thing I knew, Trask was out of the Secret Service and I was out of the Army, and the Army was after me. That's when I went looking for Trask."

"Trask got you kicked out of the Army?"

"Don't know."

"What do you mean you don't know, Addie's told me you were one of the few Trask ever let into his inner-sanctum, so to speak," Martin said.

"Yeah, he found me while I was on the run. He hid me and sent some jobs my way."

"What did he tell you when you asked him?"

"I never asked him," Jacob answered.

"You mean to tell me that Trask might have gotten you kicked out of the Army and put your life on the line and you didn't ask him why?" Martin said slowing the car as the traffic into the city became heavier.

"That's right, what good would it do to have another person after me, especially one like Trask. Martin, have you ever heard the old saying keep your friends close and your enemy's closer?"

"It's one of Addie's favorite sayings, so was Trask a friend or an enemy?"

"I never did spend much time trying to figure it out I just took what he offered. When I wanted a job, I'd call on him. We would have a couple of drinks I tell you what, that man knew his whiskey, wine, cognac, and Armagnac. Do you know he has a bottle down in that cellar worth over one hundred thousand dollars? His collection of whiskey is unsurpassed and he's still collecting. Oh sorry, I got off the subject. Like I was saying, we'd have a couple of drinks and a great cigar then just like he could read my mind he'd hand me an envelope with the details of a job. That's how it worked. Who knows, maybe he took me into his confidence because I never asked."

"The more I learn about Solomon the more questions I have," said Martin.

"Lesson one Martin, leave the questions behind. When you need to know you will, and the rest is just noise," Jacob answered, reaching over to shut off the GPS. "At the next street take a left, then half way up the block on the right is the art gallery. We should be the last ones to come in. Park in front on the street wait, for the door man to come open your door," Jacob instructed.

"Are you serious? I can open my own door," Martin answered.

"Not this time. Today you are playing the part of a very wealthy man who wants to be waited on. Got it?"

"Got it, I think I can play spoiled."

"One more thing, pull the brim of your hat down a little and look down at the ground. There are cameras all around us and nothing good could come from showing our faces to the enemy," Jacob told him.

"Got it, I'm starting to like this cloak and dagger stuff," Martin answered. Following Jacob's lead, they were escorted to the gallery's show room. Immediately they were ushered to the sitting area and offered drinks. They had just received their drinks when they spotted a tall, lanky, blond woman. Her legs seemed to go on forever, unlike her skirt, as she walked directly up to Jacob, wrapped her arms around his neck and kissed him hard. Martin blushed and turned away. Then, as quickly as she had walked in, she backed away and softly slapped his cheek.

"I know, I'm sorry, it's been so long babe. I promise I'll make it up to you, if I live through this job."

"You will if you know what's good for you. Who is this sweet blushing man another stray Solomon Inc. picked up?" Krystal asked, moving closer to Martin. He immediately backed up as she entered his personnel space.

"Back off sweetheart, you're stuck with me. This is the Boss's husband and you know the Boss doesn't share her licorice or her men," Jacob warned.

"Does he have a name?" Krystal asked, standing her ground.

"I do, I'm Martin, and it's nice to meet you."

"Krystal, but Jacob here just calls me Kry because he says I cry too much, but don't listen to him, he's only seen me cry once."

"Why?" Martin asked.

"Have you ever been shot?" Krystal asked.

"No," Martin replied, surprised at the question.

"God forbid you ever do, but if you ever do, do not cry in front of this man."

"Miss Krystal, I'd cry if I got shot too. For heaven sakes Jacob, she's a lady and getting shot," Martin said.

"First of all, Martin, I can assure you that Krystal is no lady and heaven had nothing to do with it," Jacob said, earning him a dirty look and a punch to the shoulder.

"Honey, not in front of the guests," Jacob scolded, rubbing his shoulder.

"Follow me," Krystal said. Without waiting for a reply, she led them to her private office. There, in the middle of the floor, was the crate.

"Nick, are you all right in there?" Martin called out, quickly crossing the room to the crate.

"What in God's name is he doing Jacob? And who is Nick?" Krystal asked.

"Martin, is that you? Man, get me out of here. This is worse than the airplane closet," They heard Nick's voice faintly through the crate.

"My God, that's a child's voice! You have a child locked in a crate?" Krystal moved to her desk and pressed a button. Before Martin could answer the question, a man appeared at the door to the office. The expensive suit he wore couldn't hide the massive muscles underneath.

"You called?" He asked.

"Sebastian, please hurry and find me a crow bar, we have to open this crate, there's a child inside!" Krystal said.

"A child?" Sebastian repeated, giving Martin and Jacob a dirty look. Moving to the crate, he laid a massive hand on the lid, braced himself against the bottom, and pulled hard. Martin and Jacob watched as the wood creaked and the nails gave way. He repositioned his hand and pulled at the other side. Again, they heard a screeching sound as the wood gave up its nails. When he had one side completely opened, he stopped and peered in. "Boy, take my hand," He said, dropping his big hand down into the crate. Nick hung on as the big man pulled him up, sitting him on the top of the crate.

Nick wiped the sweat from this forehead and swung his legs over the side of the crate. Holding on to the man's arm, he slid down like he was climbing down a tree. "You're the wrong color to be the hulk, but I sure am glad to be out of there," Nick said. Looking up at his new friend, he suddenly felt like one of the ants he liked to step on in the garden.

"Come here you sweet little man. Hey, you two knew he was in there?" Krystal said. She moved towards Nick, bent down and scooped him up, holding him close. "Don't you worry, I'm going to get you safely up to Solomon and get you a cold drink and a nice treat from the bakery. You two are lucky I don't have my gun on me or I'd shoot you both. Who puts a boy in a box!"

"Calm down honey, Nick is no boy," Jacob realized when he said it he was in for another sharp reprimand.

"Not a boy? Then what is he, a genie in a bottle?"

"Tell me sweet little man, would you grant me a wish?" Krystal asked.

"Sure, if I can," Nick answered. He looked over at Martin and Jacob, smiling as he snuggled close to Krystal.

"What I mean is yes, he is a boy, but right now he's on a job with us and we had to smuggle him in somehow."

"Somehow? You guys put Ray in a bakery truck and the boy in a create?" Krystal demanded.

"That's what I told them, but who listens to a kid?" Nick said.

"Why you little," Jacob said, making a move toward him only to be stopped by a massive arm that came out of nowhere.

"Not on my watch," was all Sebastian said.

"Why you gonna shoot me?" Jacob asked. Martin moved closer to Nick and Krystal, who nodded and smiled in his direction.

"No, I'm gonna snap you like a twig," Sebastian answered, moving closer to Jacob.

"Krystal, call off your pit bull!" Jacob said.

"Why? I'd like to see him throw you around a couple of times."

"Ma'am, you don't want Mr. Sebastian to mess up his suit or get blood on it. My mom get's real mad when I mess up my dress clothes," Nick added.

"You sweet thing, your mother is right," said Krystal.

"Sebastian, leave us. I'll get them up to Solomon, this boy needs to eat," instructed Krystal. With a grunt and a sneer at Jacob, he left them.

"Follow me," Krystal said. No one said a word as they followed. Jacob was trying to get a hand on Nick, who stayed very close to Krystal's side. "Right this way,"

"Lady, we can't walk through walls," said Nick.

"No? Let me show you how this works," Krystal said. She reached over to a picture hanging on the wall. "Do you like this picture little man?"

"It's okay, I like horses," said Nick. He watched her slide her fingers along the side of the picture frame. There was a soft clicking sound and then the whole wall opened up, revealing a stair case. "Wow, can I?" Nick asked.

"Go on ahead Mr. Ray should be waiting for you at the top," Krystal told him. Nick wasted no time and raced past her up the steps. Jacob stepped forward, put his hand around her waist, and pulled her close.

"Go ahead Martin, Ray should be keeping guard. I'll be right there."

"You certainly will," Krystal said, pushing him away. She gave Jacob a good shove through the door as it closed behind him.

"I think she's pissed. She didn't even turn on the lights for us. Nick, are you okay up there?" Martin called out.

"Let there be light," said Jacob, pushing the button. "Don't worry Martin, she's always like this. Once we have a break in the case, I'll take her to bed and buy one of her paintings, and then she'll be just fine."

"I almost believe you," Martin said and laughed.

"You know what Martin Addie did all right with you," Jacob said as they walked up the long stairs.

"Thanks Jacob. I think," When they reached the top, they looked down the hallway and noticed that a door was standing wide open.

"Down there. This hall goes between the art gallery and Solomon's offices," Jacob told him, stepping ahead to lead the way.

CHAPTER 13

On the screen, as Debbie and Angus watched, Wolff pulled out Addie's chair and sat down next to her. Isaac stood first and reached across the table to shake Wolff's hand. Wolff couldn't believe he was seeing Isaac and could feel him shake his hand.

"Good to see you again Wolff, it's been too long," Isaac said. The grip of his handshake and the sound of his voice were as strong and clear as ever, thought Wolff as he shook back.

"It's good to see you too Boss. I've missed our cigar talks and chess games. You're looking good, I mean," Wolff said, letting go of his hand.

"You mean for a dead man? You're looking good too, my boy. I bet you do miss my whiskey. Do you remember Special Agent Trask?" Isaac asked.

"I do Sir," Wolff said, turning to shake Trask's hand.

"Well, I owe my whiskey collection to him and his 'distributors', wasn't that what you called them old man?" Isaac said. He smiled over at Trask who was still holding on to Wolff's hand. His steel blue eyes were staring deep into Wolff's, who stared back and tried to study the old man, who was clearly studying him.

"He called you an old man. Are you going to take that from him?" Wolff asked, pulling his hand back.

"It's a private joke between us. We were born on the same day, just two minutes apart," Trask answered.

"I had to pull him out then, just like I had to pull him around this whole project. Trask, where's your manners, get us a round of your best," Isaac said.

"Wait a minute you had to pull him out? What do you mean by that?" Addie asked.

"I'll answer your question with a question. Did you ever wonder why a Secret Service Special Agent would have been asked to join a military project like W.I.S.E?" Trask asked.

"I just thought they were covering all the bases or that you had a degree like Pike's that made you valuable to the project," Addie answered.

"I had a special talent we both did, just like you and Wolff. But Isaac and I had something that you and Wolff don't have," Trask said.

"What's that?" Addie asked.

"We have what Marie called the synced power of two, similar to how your phone and your car sync up. We both have abilities and then together we have more abilities because we're...," Trask started to say when he was interrupted by Isaac.

"Because we are fraternal twins, we know what to do and agree together, without speaking. It seems to make things happen faster. You remember where two or three are gathered in my name and agree...," Isaac answered.

"Fraternal twins? Why didn't you ever tell any of us? My God Isaac, was that why you were so sure Trask had been murdered?" Addie asked.

"I was sure because...," Isaac started to say.

"He was sure because I told him, just the way I'm telling you both now. Isaac and I were both murdered, but before we go any deeper Isaac is right, we need a drink," Trask said.

"He gets carried away I always have to remind him," Isaac told them.

"We can drink over here?" Wolff asked.

"Pick up your glass I have a toast to make," As they picked up the empty glasses in front of them, they filled with a clear brown liquid. Wolff did a double take as he watched the glass fill from the bottom up, slowly, as if someone unseen was pouring. "Where was I now? Oh yes, to the final victory and the continuation of our legacy through the next

99

generation," Trask toasted. Wolff couldn't tell if it was a statement or a question. When he lifted the glass to his lips and took the first drink, he couldn't believe it he never had anything like it before.

"Wow, that's the best whiskey I've ever tasted, what is it?" Wolff asked, looking over at Trask.

"You can't buy it. Let's just say its heavens best, made exclusively for you," Trask answered.

"How can that be?" Wolff asked.

"Next lesson Mr. Wolff. You see, here is the beginning of the wisdom God allowed Solomon to see. The first thing he showed Solomon was how to call into being that which is unseen. Isaac made the request for a drink to toast and I agreed. The unseen produced the glasses and the drink. Now, because all of us have different taste buds, the unseen took the request and filled each glass with a drink that tasted the best to each person, thus allowing me to serve you what you considered the best," Trask explained.

"You can't be serious. You expect me to believe that you just say it and it happens?" Wolff demanded.

"Yes, it's as good a place to start as any. You see, the lesson that God taught Solomon was to call it from nothing, and if you are in me, you will not only receive it, but it will be good. Let there be light, and there was light, and God saw it and it was good," Trask explained.

"Can anyone do it?" Wolff asked.

"Those who believe they can and are walking in the light. Go ahead Wolff, pour the next round," Trask encouraged as the others watched.

"You said you had to be a believer and walk in the light that doesn't describe me. I've done more than my share of what falls under sin, from lying to killing and everything in between," Wolff answered solemnly.

"It makes no difference what you've done, not to God. Your debts have already been paid. I don't know your soul's status Mr. Wolff and that's not for me to know however, I do know the status of your spirit and that you've been chosen, or in King Solomon's time you would be known as anointed," Trask answered.

"How do you know that?" Wolff asked.

"Because Mr. Wolff, our Mr. Trask can see the mark on your forehead," said a voice from out of the shadows. Wolff turned in the direction of the voice and a man stepped forward. His hair was dark and wavy; he stood about six feet four, had broad shoulders, and was lean and fit. He was wearing jeans and a T-shirt and carried a gold goblet in his hand. "Go ahead Mr. Wolff, pour another round. I prefer wine myself," The man said, lifting his glass.

"That's an order Sailor, you aren't getting any younger all things are possible," Isaac said sternly.

Wolff sat up a little straighter in his chair out of habit as he recognized the voice of his commanding officer and without hesitation said out loud. "Another round of Whiskey and some wine for my new friend," Immediately the glasses filled.

"Ask and yea shall receive," Trask added.

They toasted and drank. Wolff watched as the man studied him and did not take a chair. Wolff looked around the table, there was one chair left, and no one was speaking.

"Aren't you going to introduce me to our new team member?" Wolff asked, nodding toward the man. Isaac started to stand, but the stranger motioned for him to remain seated.

"Mr. Wolff, who would you say that I am?" The man asked.

"I have no idea who the partners would...," Wolff started to say. He looked over at Addie, who seemed to know the man.

"Well?" The man said, taking another drink from his chalice.

From beside the empty chair next to Wolff he heard a clear husky voice from the shadows. As he turned to look, he saw one of the most impressive men he had ever seen. He too was tall, around six three, was older than the man already at the table. His black hair was streaked with white and he had extremely broad shoulders, which Wolff thought were needed to hold up his huge arms. This man dressed in cameo, and was no doubt a military man. As he stepped into the circle Wolff couldn't help but notice the sword that hung from his waist. It was like none he'd ever seen and it appeared to be very heavy, yet the man didn't seem to notice its weight. In his other hand, he held a chalice similar to the younger mans.

"Father," The younger man said, "anointed or not, I don't think…"

"Neither did my Father, but that's where it ceases to be our business and becomes the business of God. Now then, shall we get on with it or would you like to enquire of God before we begin?" The older man asked.

"You're right Father, forgive me," the younger man answered, bowing his head slightly in the direction of the older man.

"Then no more games, tell the man your name," The older man demanded.

"I am Solomon, King Solomon," The younger man said without offering his hand to Wolff. The older man next to Wolff poked him with his elbow.

"Don't take offense we don't shake hands as you do. It's a force of habit, too many things could be spread by touching in my day," He explained to Wolff.

"Wait, if he is King Solomon and he just called you father," Wolff said, looking over at the older man standing beside him.

"I am David, a solider like yourself, have you heard of me?" David asked.

"Yes, in Sunday school when I was a kid and when I was in the Navy," Wolff answered.

"I don't know what this Sunday school is, and I'm quite sure you were never a small goat, so sit and tell me what you learned about me from your Navy studies," David said. He then pulled out the chair next to him and sat down.

"Father," Solomon started to say, while also sitting down across from them.

"Silence, I need to know what this man knows of me, and then I will be equipped to lead him."

"Lead him? You're going to lead us?" Addie asked shaking her head. She couldn't believe what she hearing.

"He," Solomon started to say.

"He is not your concern, he is mine to lead," David answered.

"Yours to lead?" Wolff asked. He looked around the table at the others who were nodding back at him.

"I'm a fellow soldier, not one of your prize bulls," Wolff answered, folding his arms across his chest.

"As I thought, you see father, he won't be lead," Solomon said.

David ignored Solomon as he reached over with an iron grip. He laid his hand on Wolff's shoulder and turned him until he was facing him. Wolff had never felt anything like it. He was powerless, this man with one hand was turning him like he was a doll. At that moment, it was like the King and Wolff were the only two in the room, like time had slowed down to a crawl.

"Sir, in this battle I am your King and it is the King that leads the army, no matter if it is an army of one or an army of thousands, the King always leads. Do we have and understanding?" David asked.

Struggle as he might he could not get free of David's grip or move his body away. Both men locked eyes and neither flinched.

"I don't have a King," Wolff said, not knowing how David would react.

"Soldier, you remind me of myself when I was your age. Now, let me impart just a little of my wisdom to you, we all have a King. I answer to 'I Am' and for this fight solider you need someone who knows how to fight beside you in this world or...,"

"Or what?" Wolff asked, hearing a sharp intake of air from Addie behind him.

"Did they teach you about my predecessor in that Navy of yours?" David demanded.

"They did, they taught us his battle plans and how he fell from favor with God," Wolff answered,"

"You see 'I Am' anoints when he knows there is fertile ground in your heart. The 'or what' as you put it, is for him to decide. You have free will Mr. Wolff, use it to accept his anointing and fight beside me, or if 'I Am' speaks the word I will kill you now or he will. Anointed or not, anyone can be replaced, just as I was Saul's replacement," David answered him.

Wolff wasn't sure if he meant it or not. Then again, everything he knew of King David was that he lived by his word and killed thousands without hesitation and he was the only one in the room who was armed, as far as Wolff knew.

"What say you, no tongue to speak? I will have an answer. Fight alongside me or die," King David demanded an answer with such authority that Wolff, for the first time, felt himself shake.

"I'll fight beside you. It's not a good day to die. That is on one condition," Wolff answered.

"Praise God, I was hoping you would see it my way, I like you boy. What is your condition? A woman perhaps? What are you requesting?" King David said. He let go of Wolff's shoulder, sat back, and laughed a hearty laugh.

"The death of Galan by my hand," Wolff answered.

King David laughed again. "Son, that's why you're here, that's what the anointing is for, are we in agreement then?"

"Agreed, so, while we're fighting and killing Galan, what's everyone else going to be doing?" Wolff said, rubbing his shoulder.

"Fighting with us, but in a different way, Solomon and Addie need our cover so that Solomon can pass on the wisdom of God to Addie as it was passed on to him. It's time for it to be used on earth again. Addie is anointed for that," David answered.

"Wait, I thought I was anointed?" Wolff asked.

"Father, let me take this one," Solomon said. King David nodded in his son's direction.

"Mr. Wolff, my Father was anointed King because at that time in Israel's history there were battles to be fought and many to be killed in the process. I was anointed to carry the knowledge of God to build the temple and judge fairly. I didn't have the blood my father had on his hands. Addie doesn't have blood on her hands like you do. You fight to protect her and Solomon Inc. and she will carry out her work to prosper, control, and carry out Gods will for those that the father brings across her path."

"Your father killed thousands of men, but both Addie and I have killed like him in the line of duty," said Wolff.

"It wasn't the thousands of men I killed in the line of duty that took the building of God's temple away from me. It was the one innocent man that didn't die by my hand, but by my word, so that I could have his wife. That is what kept me from fulfilling my greatest dream," David answered. The sadness was clearly heard in his voice.

"And it was my wives that were not Israelites that worshiped other gods that caused the wisdom of God to be hidden away from my decedents. Then came Isaac," Solomon explained, looking over at Isaac.

"Wait a minute, first you tell us Isaac and Trask are twins, and now you're telling us they're your descendants?" Addie asked.

"From the line of David," King David interjected. All eyes turned to the founders.

Outside the room Debbie watched and listened, amazed as Angus kept an eye on the monitors and recorders to ensure everything was being captured.

"How can we be seeing and hearing them? My God, I'm seeing King David and King Solomon alive," Debbie said.

"I'll explain later," Angus told her.

"We first found out about our lineage when our great uncle Ezra died. A few days after the funeral, I was contacted by an attorney who advised me to come and claim my inheritance," Isaac said.

"Just *your* inheritance? Don't you mean yours and Trask's?" Wolff asked.

"No, it was just his. Isaac was the anointed one, I was his back up," Trask answered.

"Just as now the torch is passed to the two of you. Addie is the keeper of the keys and ring, as Solomon was, and Wolff you're her backup," Isaac said.

"But why couldn't the two of you continue at Solomon Inc.? I miss you Isaac," Addie said.

Isaac reached over and touched her arm. As he made contact, Wolff saw the faintest glow of colored lights come together a deep rose color flowed from Isaac's hand as it touched the light lavender color of Addie's arm. Together they formed a deep wine color that pulsed slightly like a heartbeat.

Before Isaac could answer, King David said, "Because woman, just like us they let down their guard and the enemy who is constantly watching slipped in."

"So, he slipped in, that still doesn't answer my question. Why did Isaac and Trask have to die? Why not just get rid of the threat?" Addie pressed.

"Do all the women in your time question authority like this one?" David asked Wolff.

106

"Yeah, only now they are upfront and in your face, unlike the ones in your time that were in the shadows manipulating the throne," Wolff said, all the while looking the King in the eye.

"Mr. Wolff, you and Father are both wrong. This has nothing to do with the women of one time or another. This goes back to Eve. The serpent chose Eve because God had not talked directly to Eve about the tree of life, so if he could convince her to eat," Solomon said.

"She got Adam to eat. I know the story, stop stalling and tell me why they had to die instead of killing the infiltrator," Addie demanded.

"We tried to kill them," Isaac said.

"But they were too strong. Wolff set them back a little when he took out Bright Star, but it wasn't enough. They, the fallen, had contacts in the physical, Henry and his Nephew Ellis and Bright Star were all in our realm," Trask said.

"I still don't understand," Addie said.

"You will know when you need to know," David answered.

"I need to know now! The rest of you can keep to yourself and play your stupid male games all you want, but I will know now why they had to die," Addie demanded, standing. As she did, the King stood too, placing his hand on his sword. He towered over Addie, but she stood her ground.

"Woman, how will you know if I choose not to tell you?" David bellowed.

"You forget King, I'm New Testament, a daughter and heir to the throne of the most high God with permission to come boldly before his thrown to make my petitions known. I command you to tell me in the name of Jesus, another of your heir's and one I believe you answer to," Addie ordered him. She moved closer to the king, so close that Wolff wondered if he could even get a knife blade between them.

King David glared at her and huffed out a breath of air. Wolff looked over and nodded toward King Solomon.

Solomon didn't say a word he just smiled and nodded back. Wolff shot him another hopeful look, nodding again toward David. Solomon waved his hand as though to say go ahead. Wolff didn't wait any longer. He stood up behind King David who turned sideways, looking back and forth between the two.

"Permission to speak Sir?" Wolff asked, cringing at the words he swore he'd never speak again.

"Speak," was all King David said.

"Unless it is a matter of the security, you might as well tell her and get it over with. We're wasting time and this woman will not give up. At times, Addie can out last any donkey," said Wolff. Before Addie could say anything, both Kings laughed.

"Woman, I believe your man called you an ass, a stubborn ass," King David said.

"I'd fight him for that, but he's right," Addie said, smiling a wicket smile at Wolff who knew this wasn't the end of that conversation.

"It's King David to you woman," David bellowed down at Addie.

"I told you, Jesus is my King," Addie retorted back without flinching.

"She's getting angry," Wolff warned.

"If she had read any of my Psalms she would know that I warned against unbridled anger. Solomon, what say you? Is the information requested a threat to the battle?" David demanded.

"No father, I'd tell her before she tries to do you in with your own sword," Solomon answered.

"Calm yourself and sit woman, it makes my head hurt to look down like this," He watched as Addie backed up and took her seat. Once she was seated David resumed shaking his head. "They had to die so they could come to this side to hold Bright Star at bay and fight the Generals advances. The enemy cannot access or control the wisdom or prevent its use now," David explained.

"Why now? It's waited all these years buried in whatever cave you left it in," said Addie, glaring at Solomon.

Solomon stood, leaned forward, and placed his palms on the table to look her in the eye.

"We don't have time for these games. Wisdom was once loose on the earth to be used by my people through me. It was then removed and yes hidden until the right time which is this time, the time of transference," He said. He then stood and started pacing on his side of the table.

"You're telling me the second coming is..." Addie said.

"Close, very close," David answered.

"But for prophesy to be fulfilled certain events have to take place like the rebuilding of God's temple," Solomon explained as he continued to pace.

"The money and military strength need to be there in order for that to happen, and it has to transfer from..." said Addie.

"From the Kings of the earth to the followers of the heavenly King. Is that enough of an answer for you woman? We don't have time to waste," said Solomon, returning to the table.

"So, it's begun," Addie said. She sat back in her chair and Wolff watched as her shoulders slumped.

"Woman, he has gifted us with strength for battle. God has given me the power to subdue under my hand those who rise up against us," King David said, laying a hand on Addie's shoulder.

"Psalm 18:39, King," Addie added.

"Indeed, it is woman, so now let us inquire of God and plan our first battle," David answered, smiling over at her with a look that would melt any woman.

CHAPTER 14

Jacob and Martin were the last to enter the office area that was Solomon Inc. Panama. As they did, they noticed everyone standing around someone or something, while several people were all talking at once.

"Hey, you guys weren't supposed to start the party without us," Jacob called out. The talking died down as he and Martin approached the circle.

"Who you got in the circle of torment Ray man?" Jacob asked Ray, stepped aside for them to see. Both Jacob and Martin stopped in their tracks when they saw Tan in the middle with Nick and Lilly in front of him holding hands. Tan and Nick looked defiant and Lilly was shaking and holding tight to Nick.

"Hey, what are you guys doing here? Lilly, come over here and tell me all about it," Martin said.

"They made Lilly feel bad," Nick said. "What kind of team is that?"

"What kind of team? I'll tell you what kind of team, one where children are not part of it!" said Ray. "Tan, what were you thinking? Addie is going to be furious, one kid is one too many, now I got two that need watching?" Ray shouted out and started to pace.

"Hey man, these are not just any kids, they're well trained kids. I will watch them and you leave Addie to me," Tan spat back at him.

"Yeah, what Tan said, don't you make my Lilly feel bad, she's very smart and very good with computers, she can be a big help to...," Nick said, standing right in front of Ray while Lilly held on tight to Martin.

"Why you little....," Ray said, reaching down to grab Nick by the collar. Tan had his hand on Ray's before he touched Nick, batting it away.

"I told you they're *my* responsibility," Tan said sternly.

"Right now, I'm the Boss on this side of the operation, is that clear?" Ray said his face less than an inch away from Tan's.

"Understood, you now have two new operatives. Direct away Boss," Tan answered.

"Lilly, tell me why you're here," Martin said. He bent down next to her and pulled her up on his knee.

Lilly looked over at Tan, wiped her eyes, sat up straight and said, "Nick and I are a team and I just couldn't let him be down here alone. Elizabeth told me he missed me." Then she smiled over at Martin. "Besides, Holly needs me too. With Nick out helping you guys, whose gonna help Miss Holly?"

"Well there you have it Ray, you need Nick and Tan, and Holly needs Lilly," Martin said standing up.

"Damn it," said Ray as he walked away from the group. Before he reached the door, he called back over his shoulder, "Holly, take Lilly with you. Same plan only now you have a second set of hands, but keep her out of sight. Tan, you help with the search. Bring anything, and I do mean anything, no matter how small or insignificant you think it might be and give it to Holly. We need to clean this place and get back to the compound as soon as we can."

As he watched, they all dispersed. Tan took Nick with him. Watching them was amazing they would have this place picked clean in no time. *Ellis, we're going to find out what you were up to and when we do, it's just too bad I can't kill you again.* Ray thought.

"Hey Tan, look at this," said Nick. At Tans direction, he had been flipping through books on the shelf in what served as a conference room and library.

"What is it?" Tan asked, taking the piece of paper Nick handed him.

"Looks like one of those Sudoku puzzle things. Addie told me once Mr. Trask loved them even before everyone

111

else knew about them. She used to say he got her hooked on them."

"He was, but not the way you think Nick. Young man, you have no idea what you've found. Hurry, we need to go through all these books, we need to flip through all the pages because they might not be loose like this one was, but first show me the book you found this in."

Nick picked up the book in the pile he started to show him, as Tan was calling for Holly and Lilly to come in.

By the time Holly and Lilly got there, Nick and Tan had found three more books. He looked up when the girls came into the room.

"Holly, look what Nick found," Tan told her smiling.

Holly walked quickly to the table, picking up the loose pieces of paper and looking at those attached inside the books that were laid out on the table.

"Are these in some kind of order?" She asked Tan.

"Look at the binders on them," he answered, "Notice how this one ends with a couple of missing numbers?"

"Yes, but..." Holly started to say, but Tan cut her short.

"Now look at the binding on the book next to it."

"It's the missing answer from the first puzzle, are they all like this?" She asked the excitement unmistakable in her voice.

"They are, but what it means I have no clue," Tan answered.

"We'll figure that out later. Lilly, you help Nick while Tan and I get pictures of these," Holly said. Before she could start, Snoop's voice came through loud and clear.

"No computers, we still don't know how much of our system has been compromised. Just box them up and get them back to the compound. We'll analyze them later."

"You got it," said Tan.

"We got what?" Ray called from the doorway.

"We got gold boss, actually Nick did," Tan called out.

"Box it up, Bird and Bat found some interesting records that are all in paper, just like these. That tells me one thing."

"Trask didn't trust the computers," Holly answered.

"Yeah, and if it's that bad, let's get as much of this packed up as we can. We need to rotate so we don't cause suspicion. I'll send Martin and Jacob out first," Ray said, turning to leave.

"Hey, if Martin and Jacob are leaving, does that mean I have to get back in the crate?" Nick asked

"Nope, not this time kid. This time you get to hide under a bakery cart. Jacob's lady friend would never let us put you back in the crate. Besides now there are two of you."

"Thank God," Nick sighed.

CHAPTER 15

Debbie watched and listened in amazement as King David and King Solomon laid out one plan after another, while the others nodded in agreement. The clocks were to be brought and placed in a circle around the chairs that held Addie and Wolff's bodies.

As Solomon explained, once the clocks were in place, the platform they surrounded would become a portal for the team to pass freely from one world to the next. The problem was that once in place, without the proper guardians fully armed by prayer, the evil ones could also pass through.

"What can they do to us if they get out?" Wolff asked.

"You saw once, a couple of years ago in New Orleans, did you not?" Asked David.

"That was one of them? But if it takes the clocks and the keys to open the portal, how did it get out?" Wolff asked.

"Bright Star, wasn't it?" Answered Addie.

"Yes, let me explain. Portals can be opened by people working together, one opening the door and allowing the entity to use his body. Another person acts as the door or portal. Both are out of body, as the two of you are now. However, there has never been a human that accomplished it and live or came out of it unharmed," Solomon explained.

"What do you mean human? Bright Star was human and he did go through and bring that thing, whatever it was, forward," Insisted Wolff.

Solomon sighed as though Wolff couldn't understand. He looked over at his father who nodded back.

"Now is the time son, tell him," David told Solomon.

Solomon stood and started to pace.

"Solomon, let me explain," Isaac said looking over at Addie and Wolff. "Wolff, during the project, we discovered something different about several members of the original team, actually we stumbled on it quite by accident."

114

"How many times do I have to tell you, nothing is by accident in God's realm? It is by plan, his plan," David insisted adamantly.

"Yes Sir, I stand corrected. We were allowed the revelation pertaining to an anomaly in the DNA of several members of the team. Myself, Trask, Henry, and an operative whose code name was Bright Star and another, his code name was Dark, we never met him, Henry was his handler."

"What kind of anomaly?" Addie pushed.

"A gene marker unlike any our geneticists had ever seen," Isaac told them as his voice became very animated.

"So, what did you do?" Asked Wolff, "How did you figure out what it meant?"

Before Isaac could answer, Solomon answered for him.

"They went to a woman of God, who inquired of the Lord."

"And," demanded Wolff.

"And," Solomon returned sharply, leaning on the table to look Wolff in the eye. "God gave her the answer she sought."

"May I continue?" Isaac asked.

"Yes, please continue, we don't have time for this nonsense," insisted King David.

"Marie was the woman and she told Trask and me that the gen originated with the Eloy," Isaac answered. Looking over at Addie, he saw the shock register on her face. When he looked back at Wolff, all he saw was bewilderment.

"That can't be right, it can't be," Addie insisted.

"What? Who are these Eloy anyway, some weird lost tribe of some kind?" Wolff asked. As he looked around the circle at all of them, they were all looking back at him like he should already know. "What?" He asked again.

Addie laid a hand on Wolff's arm and he turned to look at her. "Not a weird or lost tribe, some believe they were angels, angels that mated with women."

"You can't be serious, this is crazy, then again this whole thing is crazy. You're trying to tell me that angels came down, got it on with human women and had babies?" Asked Wolff. Looking around the room he saw everyone nodding back at him.

"It only seems crazy to you because you have never experienced them or been taught about them, but they were beings with special powers. The Eloy, for instance, were seers. The Nephilim were giants, while in my time," King David started to say.

"Stop, just stop, I give up, just tell me what this all has to do with right now?" Looking over at Addie he could see she was lost in thought.

"One of the traits that passed down was the ability to know, to walk in or see both worlds," Solomon explained.

"You mean like what we are experiencing right now? Isaac, do I have the gene? Is that why you asked me to join Solomon?" Asked Addie.

"You, Bat, Wolff and Holly," Isaac answered. "We didn't get time to test everyone, but I'll wager if we test them there will be several others."

"There you go again forgetting about this old man, your best mate, Old Salt," said the deep soft voice Addie knew so well. She found herself standing, straining to see who was behind the voice in the shadows.

"Papa Time, is that you?" Asked Addie, her voice almost pleading.

"It is child," He answered as he walked forward from the shadows. Addie ran to meet him, pulling him close.

"Papa, are you alright? What happened? Ray said he found you in your shop."

"Dead, it's ok child, go ahead and say it. You and I know it's just the start of a new life."

"I know, but I need you. Who killed you Papa?" Addie pleaded, wiping a tear from her eye.

"The wrong side child. Little did they know, they just made it easier for me to attend the board meetings. That is, once I got cleared through and got my new body and all."

"Board meetings?" Wolff said. "So, you're on the board too?"

"This young man is dull," Solomon insisted.

"Quiet son, he is my commander of men. This is all new to him, show him respect," David commanded. Solomon sat back, crossing his arms across his chest.

"Great, so now I've heard everything. Well, I guess if you're a board member, a ghost is the way to go. After all, it's not like they can come after you or anything," Wolff said, rubbing his head.

"Isaac, so now that you and Trask are deceased are you board members?" Addie asked.

"As you said, we are dead, which means we are no longer partners in the business. You and whoever you hire to replace Ellis are the partners that answer to the board with Edmund serving as chairman."

"The IRS be hanged," Trask, who had been sitting back, puffing on his cigar stated.

"Who signs documents for the board?" Addie demanded, waving her hand at the two kings.

"We do. I sign as David King and my son signs as Solomon King. We are the King family."

"Oh my God," Addie said. She looked over at Wolff for support and noticed he was trying hard not to laugh.

"What?" Wolff said. When he saw her looking at him again, "All the IRS needs are signatures, they don't have to see bodies do they? So, who else is on the board?"

All Addie could do was shake her head. Outside the room, Debbie looked over at Angus.

"Addie, please sit," Trask added, holding out Addie's chair for her to sit.

"Don't tell us Santa Clause, I don't think Addie could take it," said Wolff.

Trask huffed, "Santa was busy, we settled for Angus and his brother Marcus."

"Wonderful, so they all knew about this and said nothing?" Addie sighed, squeezing her temples between her fingers.

"Confidentially dear girl, you can see why we would need to keep the board members identity secure, what with kidnapping and all these days," answered Trask.

"This is quite the board you have here, anyone else we know?" Wolff asked.

"We were thinking of adding Addington's friend Miss Debbie," answered Isaac.

"Me? Did that man, that dead man, say he wanted me on the board of Directors of Solomon Inc.?" Asked Debbie, Angus, noticing she'd started sliding off the side of her stool, caught her and pushed her back up.

"I suggested you my dear, you're a perfect fit. That way, almost half the board is well dead and the other half of the board is alive. Doesn't that sound good to you, good odds and all?" Debbie stared at him, not knowing what to say. When she finally collected herself, all she could say was, "This has nothing to do with odds Angus. I have no idea what would be expected of me as a member of the Board of Directors. For heaven's sake, I don't even know the business."

"We need fresh eyes and who better than to keep all of us men in line, living or dead. Yes, you are the perfect choice," said Angus. He nodded back at Debbie, who now reached over and patted his arm.

"If you think so and Addie agrees, I'll give it my best."

"Did you hear that?" Isaac said.

"Hear what?" Sighed Addie, still rubbing her head.

"We're going to have to work on your hearing," Trask answered. "It was your friend, she told Angus she would accept our offer," Addie looked over at Wolff who shrugged his shoulders and rolled his eyes in response.

118

"Okay, so let me get this straight," Addie said, looking over at Isaac, "you say several of us have this gene, so what does that mean for Solomon Inc.?"

"It means we are all part of the final phase of the plan, whatever that turns out to be."

"How do we know?" Wolff asked.

"We know because it's written, Mr. Wolff. Tell me, have you read the book lately?" David asked.

"By the book, are you talking about the Bible?" Asked Wolff rolling his eyes.

"I am, in the book of revelation the battle plan is drawn, several seals have already been broken and the horses have been dispatched. That's why you are here, to carry out part of the plan behind the scenes," David explained.

"Which part would that be, or don't you know?" Wolff asked.

"Mr. Wolff, the Lord God has his own time and ways. He reveals what he needs to, when he needs to. When I was building the temple and encountering the demons, I discovered several of them wandering the earth with the sole purpose to distract and confuse humans. One of the ways they accomplished their goal was to keep men's minds controlled by the past, or by concerning themselves with a future that may never come to pass," Solomon told him.

"What you're telling me is God wants our minds on the battle of the day. Funny thing, that was part of my past military training, right Addie?" Wolff answered.

"And where do you think your trainers got it from?" Trask interjected, "What they didn't tell you is that the Bible and many of the other writings have been studied for years by the top military leaders of our time. More battle plans have been drawn up using the God's battle plans than anything man has come up with."

"There is nothing new under the sun, is that what you're telling me?" Said Wolff.

"You have read my writings, splendid! There may be hope for you yet," Solomon interjected, smiling at Wolff for the first time.

"We can't stay much longer," said Addie. "Who is in charge and what's next?" Addie watched as Trask, Isaac and Papa Time turned to look at King David.

"My son and I are in charge. I will lead my commander Wolff in setting up the portal and through him I will direct his men," David instructed, turning to Solomon.

"I will work with Addie and her people to assemble my book once again then train them in the use of the book and my ring," Solomon told them.

"To what end? What is our mission?" Addie asked.

"To do what God instructs, when he instructs it. For now, you have your orders," David answered.

"You said you would instruct us, but how? Do we have to keep coming back here like this?" Asked Wolff.

"No, from the time the meeting started, data pertaining to frequencies, energy emissions the likes of which I don't understand, have been collected and run into one of Pike's special boxes. Angus is monitoring the computers as we speak. Pike will compile the data and transfer it to Snoop. Once Pike works his magic, you will be able to communicate with us like you do the rest of the team," Trask explained.

"So that's why you had Pike and Angus come down here. They were helping you set this up," said Addie.

"They were preparing for battle, like God prepared me in the Sheppard's field. It takes a lot of preparation if we're going to slay these philistines and come home with their heads," David said.

"How do we come home with demon heads?" Asked Wolff.

"We don't, we control them. We use them and then bind them for as long as God tells us to," Solomon answered.

"How long is that?" Wolff asked.

"No one knows the day and the time but God himself," said Addie. Everyone around the table nodded back.

"I move to close this board meeting," said Isaac.

"I second that motion. Addie, Wolff, you've been gone a long time. Walk slowly back through the door, eat and drink everything Angus gives you, before trying to get out of your chair. Then get some rest before you try and meet with the rest of your group. By then, they will all be back at the compound ready for your orders. In other words dismissed!" Isaac instructed.

Addie looked over at Wolff who nodded back. They had their orders and had been dismissed. They stood, looked around the table at the others watching them. Addie led the way and walked toward the door, Wolff followed close behind. No way was he getting left behind with these guys.

Wolff awoke with a start; his whole body was shaking uncontrollably. Debbie was at his side, he was wrapped in what looked like a foil blanket that he could feel starting to warm up.

"Welcome back," She said as she undid the restraints around his hands. As he rubbed his wrists, he felt them start to warm.

Just as Isaac had told them, he watched as Debbie moved a tray table, like the ones used in hospitals, in front of him. There was food and several small glasses of fluid.

"I have to eat and drink all this?" Wolff asked.

"I have my orders," answered Debbie, "you eat and drink it all before I let you stand up,"

Wolff looked over at Addie and noticed that she was way ahead of him. Debbie lifted the lid off the plate. Once the smell reached his nostrils it was like he hadn't eaten in months. He forgot about everything else but eating. With each bite, he was amazed at the taste it was like he could taste every ingredient. As he finished, he patted his lips with his napkin and looked over at Debbie.

"Wow, for a man that was asking if he had to eat it all, you sure made short work of it. Do you want seconds?" Asked Debbie, pulling the tray away.

"No ma'am, but you sure are some cook."

"Not me, Pike cooked this meal and sent it down, Angus has kept me busy," Debbie added.

"Well congratulations on your promotion to a Board member," Wolff said as he bent to help Debbie with his leg restraints.

"I didn't formally accept yet. I have to talk it over with Joe, right Addie?" Debbie said over her shoulder.

"I know, take it easy standing for the first time," Addie told Wolff as Angus joined her.

Wolff nodded back then gingerly lowered his feet to the floor, taking a hold of Addie's outstretched hand, he stood.

"Wow, this is different it reminds me of having sea legs. What do you think Addie?"

"Never thought about it, but that's a good way to put it."

Angus handed Addie and Wolff their ear buds.

"Snoop just said the team is back with some interesting information they found at the office," Angus told them.

"Solomon's book?" Both Addie and Wolff asked at the same time, looking at each other and then back at Debbie and Angus.

CHAPTER 16

"You all go ahead, I'll shut things down here and bring the discs up for the team to review," said Angus.

"I'll help you, no time like the present to learn how to do it," said Debbie. Angus smiled and headed for the equipment.

"You got your legs sailor?" Addie asked, looking over at Wolff.

"My legs are fine Boss, go," He answered, falling in behind Addie as they headed for elevators. He waited until they were inside, then pressed the red button when the doors closed.

"What?" Addie asked.

"What? Are you serious Addie? Let me see, in the last couple of weeks Solomon lost another partner, I've been kidnapped, we're all on the run from Henry, a man that was not only supposed to be a partner but was supposed to be in a coma not able to be chasing us, and now you want me to just accept that I have some rare gene linked to angels, anything else?"

"Yeah, you forgot you just crossed over into another dimension and had a board meeting with King David, King Solomon and two of our dead founders," she answered as though it was an everyday event. As she reached for the button, Wolff stopped her.

"I didn't forget, I can only wrap my head around so much at one time. Damn it Addie, you could have warned me, at least about some of it."

"No, I couldn't, they didn't tell me about you or their plans. Tonight, was all news to me too, in case you hadn't noticed my surprise."

"Okay just please, going forward, let me know when you know, deal?"

"Wolff, I know it's a lot to take in all at once. I had more time and the founders were there to guide me. There just isn't time now, you said it yourself, Henry and whoever he's working for are not only on our heels, they're out to kill us and take over Solomon. I need you to just follow orders right now. I promise…,"

Before she could finish her sentence, Wolff had her in his arms, pulling her close. Bending down, he kissed her forehead as she hugged him back. She then stepped out of his arms and smiled.

He smiled back and then set his jaw, letting Addie know he was all business now. "You got it Boss, but when this is over, all I got to say is that you will have a lot of explaining to do."

Addie didn't say anymore, she just reached for the control panel.

"What's our next stop?"

"Floor Five, I think dinner is ready," Addie answered. Suddenly, she was feeling really tired.

"Yeah, who's cooking? Everything was good except for that pasty stuff Angus gave us at the end. What was that stuff anyway?"

"Manna and a high protein drink that Trask designed based on some formulation he received during one of his trips to the other side."

"Wait, did you say Manna? Like, in the wilderness in the Bible, Manna?" Wolff asked.

"The same."

"Stop, I don't even want to know how he got his hands-on Manna. That's just too much information today," Wolff answered, holding up his hand as the doors opened.

Addie shot past Wolff her energy was coming back now. As they rounded the corner of the elevators, they heard voices. The closer they got to the voices, wonderful smells accosted their senses. Addie looked over at Wolff who was smiling at her.

"I know that dish. Next to me, Pike is the best chief I know. Suddenly, I don't know how I can be but I'm starving again. Last one to the kitchen loses," Wolff told her, passing her up.

Addie let him go. She was still hungry too, so she could only imagine how hungry he was after his first time on the other side. Besides, she knew Pike and if there was one thing she knew, not only could Pike cook, but that southern boy never let anyone go away from his table hungry. There was always enough food to feed her army. When she walked in, Martin stood and headed straight for her. He held her close until she patted his chest and whispered that she was fine, but incredibly hungry. Martin pulled out her chair as Pike set a plate and a glass of wine in front of her.

"It smells wonderful as usual Pike," Addie said. She bowed her head for a quick prayer. Pike waited until she looked up again.

"I made your favorite for desert, Granny's chocolate cake," He said. Sitting down opposite of her, he poured himself a cup of coffee from the pot on the table. "How did Wolff do down there Addie? He doesn't look any worse the wear," He said, glancing over at Wolff.

"I thought for a minute we were going to have some trouble on the other side, and then again in the elevator. Wolff will wait for answers as long as he gets them, but when this job is finished we need to train him the right way."

"That's the plan Addie girl. Now, I'll let you eat," Pike answered, nodding at Martin.

Martin let Addie take a couple of bits before he asked her anything.

"So, what happened down there honey?"

"Not much sweetheart, Wolff and I met the board of directors and Debbie got elected as a new board member," Addie said. She smiled at Martin who could only shake his head and smile back as she took another bite of Pike's incredible biscuits. Addie waited until everyone had eaten,

125

and then asked them all to follow her to the board room for a debriefing.

"Today has been a long day for everyone from what I've heard, and we have a lot of information to go over, but not tonight. Tonight, we rest and get a fresh start in the morning. We'll meet back here at 06:00 after breakfast. Ray, I want you to brief the team on what you all found at the office, and I'll fill you all in on our meeting. Our rooms are on level two below us and Snoop will give you your room assignments. Get some rest, believe me, you're going to need it. See you all tomorrow morning."

"You want me on first patrol Boss?" Austin asked.

"No need, as long as we are here and on lock down, the house watches itself. Not to mention we have our two founders hovering around," Addie answered.

They all exchanged looks around the room.

"I'll explain in the morning," said Addie.

"I can't wait to hear it," Jacob said.

"Trust me old friend, you can," Wolff said, giving Jacobs shoulder a little punch.

One by one they filed out of the room and headed for the elevator while Addie, Martin, Debbie, and Joe stayed behind with Pike.

"You need help in the kitchen Pike?" Addie asked.

"No Ma'am, it seems Trask made provisions for all the staff to stay on, with Snoop watching over them that is. I have a full kitchen staff. All I had to do was send them to market and then give directions. The kitchen was cleaned up as we were serving, and they are taking down the dining room as we speak. What I want to know, Addie girl, is who the board members are."

Addie hesitated a minute to see if there was any objection from the other side before she spoke. None came, so she answered Pike's question. "Trask, Isaac, Papa Time, Edmund, now Debbie, and let me see, oh yes, King David and his son King Solomon."

126

Pike stared at her, the last time he had been at a loss for words was the night she told him Isaac was dead and Henry was in a coma. They all waited, letting him have time to let it soak in. Pike shook his head, looking over at Addie he said. "You and Wolff opened the circle? You saw them and came back with no ill effects? Addie, did Angus monitor the two of you? We need to continue monitoring your vitals, we need to make sure."

"We're fine Pike. See, Snoop is ever watching," Addie answered, holding up her wrist for Pike to see the monitor. "We're watching Wolff closely, even though he's in great shape, he hasn't been trained or been on the recommended diet."

"Snoop, how's the tracking looking?" Asked Pike.

"No worries Pike, all is well with both our travelers," said Snoop.

"Debbie, did you see them, King David and Solomon?" Joe asked.

"I did, and you will too at the debriefing tomorrow, right Addie?"

"Yes, I bet Angus is going over the recordings with Holly right now," answered Addie. She looked over at Pike. "Pike, is there something else bothering you, besides our vitals?"

Pike looked over at her, shaking his head. "It was all theory we had so little to go on when we put the circle together. Right before we tried it for the first time, the way you and Wolff used it tonight, we got word that Bright Star had tried and failed and was barely alive. That is, if you could call it alive."

"That's what I could never figure out, how could Wolff be so sure he killed Bright Star if he was with Henry trying to cross over?" Addie asked.

"You don't know?" Asked Angus, they all turned and looked over at him walking into the room.

"Know what?" Addie asked.

127

"Why Bright Star was so deadly and no one could catch him, why he seemed to be carrying out a hit in one part of the world and blowing something up in another at the same time," Pike answered.

"And you figured it out?" Addie asked.

No, not me, Trask did, and he told Marie and Marie passed it on. You see, once Trask died and was on the other side, he could see the life cord that bound them."

"I've heard of the life cord but..," Addie started to say.

"Well I haven't, can you explain it please?" Debbie asked.

"I can dear lady, you see, we all have a life cord, one the starts at the crown of our heads that goes to the maker. Then there are others that come from our hands or hearts, to others that are in our family or those between husband and wife or lovers. They bind us together, and depending on what the attachment is, they can be different colors. Some people can see the interaction here like Addie sees and talks to those on the other side, but for those that have passed over they see the cords from that side because the cords are most visible in that plane."

"So, what did Trask see on the other side?" Addie pressed.

Angus turned to look at her. "He saw Bright Star standing half on our side in a military compound and half on his side. However, that wasn't the important part, it was the cord. He had a very strong cord leading to another man that is very much alive. Their cords were connected at the waist."

"What does that mean?" Martin, who had been very quiet until now, asked Angus.

"That they were siblings, brothers, the cord was solid and gold," Angus answered, looking from Martin to Addie.

"They were twins?" Addie asked.

"Not just twins, and not just identical twins, they were mirror twins," Angus answered.

"So, Wolff killed Bright Star's twin?" Addie asked.

"We think so. Pike and I think it was the timing of the killing that was most important. We think Bright Star could pass over to carry out his missions, or maybe aid his brother in his missions from the other side, and then come back. We believe Henry was using the brothers as his super assassins and Trask found out."

"How?" Addie asked.

"We don't know, and we also don't know how he got his hands on Bright Star," Pike answered, pinching his forehead with his fingers.

"Got his hands on Bright Star? What are you talking about?" Addie pressed.

"The man Jacob found in the nursing home," Pike answered.

"That was Bright Star?" Addie asked.

"We believe so. Isaac thought that Bright Star was on the other side helping his brother complete a job when Wolff killed him. We believe that was the reason Bright Star's mind or soul was *seared*, as the ancient writings call it. Had Bright Star been in his body when Wolff killed his twin, he may have been fine," Pike told them.

"This is too much for me," Joe said.

"Angus and I will explain more tomorrow at the briefing. I know it's a lot to take in, especially when you have never studied it, not to mention how tired we all are. Let's get some sleep," Pike told them.

"I'll second that, I'm exhausted," Joe answered.

"We all are, this can all wait until tomorrow," Addie said, leading the way to the elevators.

CHAPTER 17

Wolff held back, letting the others get off the elevator on the second level.

"Hey man, are you coming?" Jacob asked, holding the door for Wolff.

"Not yet, you go ahead," answered Wolff.

"Where are you going?" You just going to ride the elevator?"

"No, I'm going back up to get something to drink I've been thirsty ever since my walk on the wild side,"

"You feel like some company? Do you want to talk about it, or do you want to be a lone Wolff tonight?"

"Thanks man, but I need to sort this thing out. Hell Jacob, I don't know if I believe what happened or if the Founders just figured out a way to screw with everyone's minds."

"Sorry man, like it or not, this is real. You were in New Orleans, you saw it for yourself. Trask talked to me about what happened you knew Trask was a man made of steel, inside and out. I'd been in some tight spots with that man and nothing, and I mean nothing, shook him. The night that Addie and Marie called him and told him about what happened and what they saw, he was shaking, and I mean physically shaking. He hung up without a word and went straight to the wine cellar and opened that bottle of Armagnac you were drinking from tonight. I watched him drink two fingers down before he spoke. When he looked over at me, he was as pale as he could be. I'll never forget what he said. He told me the end is coming and the door had just been opened."

"He said that?"

"Yeah, and a month later he was."

"He was dead," said Wolff, finishing Jacob's sentence. Jacob nodded and stepped aside, letting the elevator doors shut. Wolff reached over and punched the main floor button. When it opened, he headed for the kitchen. As he got closer he heard Pikes voice and the laughter of a lady. *'Must be one of the maids,'* Wolff thought. When he walked in, everyone stopped talking and turned to look his way.

"May I be of help Sir?" One of the ladies asked, setting down her dish towel.

"I'm just looking for something to drink Ma'am."

"Hard or soft?" Asked Pike, standing next to the refrigerator.

"Soft this time and lots of it; ice tea if you have it I can't believe how thirsty I am after..."

"After your workout?" Pike said, tipping his head toward the ladies.

"Yeah, my workout."

"Marina, would you bring us some tea on the veranda please?" Asked Pike.

"Yes Sir, right away Sir."

Wolff let Pike lead the way to the veranda. Pike walked to the far end, away from the kitchen and curious ears. Marina brought a pitcher and two glasses to them. Wolff waited until Marina left, downed his first glass of tea, and poured another. He finished half of the second glass before setting it down.

"There is more on your mind besides tea, am I right Wolff?"

"You're damn right there is, come clean with me Pike. Did you know about that room, about the?"

"The meeting room? I did, in fact I helped design it."

"Meeting room? Those chairs, the electrodes, it's all a mind game, right? Suggestions and images pushed into our brains, but none of its real."

"Sorry Wolff, no mind games. The electrodes are only placed to record the images you are experiencing, so we can all see what you see. I know it's a lot to get a handle on without any training up front, but there just wasn't time."

"A lot to get a handle on? Pike, we're talking about leaving our bodies or whatever it is that happened to me and."

"And communicating with people who are in another plane think of it this way, they are the same people you knew here on earth, they just took off the coat that was their body and left it behind."

Pike could see the anger rising to the surface in Wolff's face.

"First lesson, don't go there Wolff. Anger is not of the light unless it is righteous anger. If you allow the anger to take hold, you feed the enemy. They will become stronger and you won't be able to fight. They want to taunt you, confuse you, cause doubt so that they can feed off that energy and hurt you or Addie. Addie needs you now Wolff."

Wolff stared at him. Then, just as Pike saw the anger in his face and tightening of his muscles, he watched Wolff slowly relax. Wolff sighed deeply, slumped back in his chair, and drank down the rest of his tea.

"So, when does the damn thirst stop?" Wolff asked.

Pike smiled back. "From now on, you and Addie will consume a drink every day that looks and tastes like an instant orange drink. It's a formula that Angus and I came up with to hold the hydration in when the cells get 'scrambled' as we called it. From here on out, the two of you will also be on a special diet that is designed to support the body as it travels from one plane to another. Angus and I will work with you every day to prepare you. When this is all over, you'll go and spend a month or two with Marie. She'll sharpen your skills and teach you how to take care of yourself going forward."

"What if I don't want to go on after this job?"

Pike leaned forward, looking Wolff in the eyes. "This isn't like any other job you've had or ever will have. You don't get it, you've been chosen since before you were born. You were marked, and the plan was already put in place.

This isn't like working for Uncle Sam. You can run, but you will never hide. Man, this is God we're talking about. Like it or not, his plan will be carried out and you are part of that plan."

"And if I say screw God, I won't do it, then what?"

"Then the demons get to have you. See Wolff, you have part of the angelic host in you. You can either choose his way or theirs. Man, if you won't stand beside Addie and follow this through, then get out of our way now and let us put Bat in. I won't take a chance on losing Addie. Not only is she too important to me, she's too important to the plan and she deserves a partner that is all-in, so make your choice."

Wolff felt himself tense again. *Damn, why him? Why this?* As much as he hated all this, he knew Pike was right he had to be all in or all out. For the first time in his life, he knew he couldn't walk away. He looked back at Pike and gave his answer.

"I'm all-in you and Addie can count on me."

"Pinky swear?" Pike asked, holding up his little finger smiling at Wolff.

"Screw you Pike, and your pinky," Wolff answered. Standing, he smiled at Pike before he turned and left. Wolff didn't look back at Pike or say another word he just walked across the veranda. He walked down the hall, got in the elevator, and pressed the button for the second floor. Tapping his ear bud, he heard Snoop's voice.

"About time you let me in. What can I do for you man?"

"I'm on the second floor," Wolff answered.

"I know where you are. Even when you're not talking to me, I always know where you are."

"I'm not in the mood to play, just tell me where my room is."

"Wow, the Wolff is growly. Good thing I chose the room I did, it's twenty-two, at the end of the hall to your right. Anything else I can do for you?"

133

"No, that's it, and Snoop."

"Yeah?"

"This room had better be legit."

"Dude, how can a room not be legit?"

"What I mean is I'm in no mood for one of your jokes. When I open this door, it better not be all pink and lacy," Wolff told him.

"No pink, no lace, I'm making notes," answered Snoop, sounding irritated.

Wolff signed and opened the door. His body suddenly felt like lead, and he was thirsty again. As he walked through the door the lights came on automatically. God, he loved this place. Snoop was right, no pink and no lace. In fact, the room was not only very masculine, it was decorated with some beautiful, and knowing Trask, priceless works of Native American art. He had to laugh when he saw the huge painting of the lone wolf on a hill. It was sitting in the snow by himself with a full moon overhead. The wolf's head was tilted back as he howled, the steam floated up from his mouth to the sky.

"Is that a laugh I hear?" Snoop asked.

"Yeah man, I love the wolf. In fact, I like all the stuff in this room."

"There is a sauna set up in the master bath. Trask had it set up like the Native American Sweats he would attend from time to time. It's infrared, so you don't put water on the stones, you just go in and meditate."

"Does it come with a pipe?" Wolff asked.

"Sorry, its bring your own," answered Snoop.

Wolff walked into the bathroom to check it out. "Man, Trask not only had great taste he had some imagination," said Wolff.

"No he didn't, he just recreated the things he saw, experienced, and liked. Imagination was the hardest lesson Marie taught him."

"Why did she have to teach him imagination?" Asked Wolff.

"I forgot you're starting at ground zero. You have to have an imagination to be able to call those things that are not, as though they are. But that's a lesson for another day. Right now, you need to sleep my man."

"Is that an order doctor Snoop?"

"It is."

Wolff nodded and pulled off his shirt. In the shower, he let the hot water cascade down over his head and down his back. He didn't want to think about anything. He finished his shower, pulled on a pair of clean shorts, and walked across the room to the bar. Grabbing a crystal glass, he scanned the bottles on the lighted shelves. He stopped at a bottle of twelve-year-old Irish whiskey, which was one of Addie's favorites, as he recalled. He took the bottle with him, sat down in one of the huge padded chair in the sitting area, and reached for the remote. He just wanted to see some mindless crap, drink some whiskey, and fall asleep.

CHAPTER 18

Martin laid awake watching Addie toss and turn. *Where was she when she slept?* He wondered if his wife ever got any down time. He turned on his side and slid up behind her, pulling her close. She moved close and was still. Martin smiled and drifted off.

Then the dream came again. She was back in New Orleans, sitting next to Isaac on the bench in front of the levee. He was telling her that he would be going away, and that he wanted her to have his pen to remember him by. She was confused. What was he saying, he was going away? Where to?

Suddenly her surroundings changed, she was in the old warehouse with Marie and something else was there with them. Out of the shadows they heard it growl.

Marie started to recite a text that Addie had never heard. The growling continued to get louder and louder; it was getting close. Marie's recitation now was louder and more forceful. Addie saw a face emerge from out of the shadows. It had red eyes, a snarling mouth, and fangs. As it came closer it grew and the stench until it filled the air around her was making her sick.

Addie heard Marie yelling from behind her. "Addie, your training! Remember your training!"

The creature snarled back. "Old woman, you're a fool to come against me with nothing but a weak woman. How dare you insult me like this. You have been a thorn in my side long enough. This is the night that you and your pitiful excuse for a student will die," the thing hissed. As Addie watched, it reached out with a clawed hand. A piece of pipe flew across the room, striking Marie in the leg. She screamed out as she dropped to the floor. "Addie, call those who frustrate!" Marie screamed.

Seeing her friend down jolted Addie into action, standing between the monster and Marie, Addie demanded the beast identify himself. He laughed, and Addie ducked out of the way as a brick flew at her head. "In the name of Jesus, tell me your name!" Addie demanded.

"You feeble excuse for a woman, you have no power over me," it hissed back and pointed a claw in Addie's direction. From behind her, Addie could hear Marie still reciting as a dark red light came at Addie from the tip of the claw. Quickly, Addie held up a hand to repel the light and began reciting what Marie had taught her.

Suddenly, she felt the warmth in her hands and saw a brilliant purple light forming around them. Addie walked straight toward the beast. As she did, she felt someone or something at her side. She glanced just long enough to see a huge being of light to her right smiling at her, he was handsome. He may not be one of her men but, somehow, she knew him. He was dressed for battle beside her. He nodded back at her and a peace filled her. Looking back quickly at the beast, she noticed that it was not advancing, but it had grown in size and intensity. Addie continued forward.

"It is written to God be the victory, I am a child of the most high God, daughter of Adam. I am redeemed by the blood of Jesus Christ and given dominion over all things on earth and all the beings of the air between the earth and heaven. I command you now to give me your name."

"I am the demon who guards the first entrance to the gate. Send away the one who frustrates!" He screamed, pointing at the being on Addie's right side.

Addie watched as the being stepped slightly forward to cover part of her side. Addie did what Marie had taught her and spoke out loud. "Holy Spirit, take my tongue and speak through me."

Feeling the warmth fill her body, she watched the being at her side take a ready position for battle. A position she and all her men had been taught when they entered the military.

The demon expanded, filling her field of vision. The murky crimson light was pulsing and swirling in front of them. "Your God sends a woman and only one soldiers to fight me?"

Addie stood her ground and opened her mouth, not knowing what would come out. When she heard her voice strong and full of authority rise up and speak, she felt her whole body shake as she pressed ahead.

"Be reminded that it is written, a Sheppard boy killed goliath with one stone. You who guard the gate, you who have come to kill the chosen ones, be bound by the angels that frustrate you. Go back to who summoned you and take your anger out on him. It was he who sent you out of time. This is not your time; the Lord God establishes the time and it is not yet come."

Then, as quickly as it had come, the warmth was gone. Addie coughed and felt sick, but kept moving forward.

"You, a weak woman, will not send me back," it hissed.

"You must go, you have no place here. By the power Jesus Christ has given me through his death and resurrection!" Addie shouted back.

A stream of red light came toward Addie and she could see a claw forming, but she stood her ground. Before the claw could touch her, the warrior standing at her side raised his sword. Stepping forward, he sliced through the smoke.

The demon yelled out in pain and shouted profanity as it moved to surround Addie. A foul stench filled the air all around her, swirling as the warrior positioned himself at her back. She saw claws coming out of the smoke, trying to grab her. Addie was nauseated; it was hard to see through the swirling mass, but she could see that this being was fighting for her.

Where was Marie? She had to get to Marie. Addie pushed and punched her way through the red smoke. As she cleared the circle, she saw Marie lying on the ground bleeding. She felt the searing blow to the side of her head and heard Marie scream.

"Save the one who is a key!"

Addie bolted right up in bed, fists punching, with Martin grabbing for her.

"Addie, it was a dream, it was only a dream, wake up! It's me, Martin, you're safe," Martin kept saying, holding on tight, rocking her in his arms.

Addie stopped fighting him; she was ringing wet. Turning to him she said, "Martin, I know now, I remember, I remember what happened that night in New Orleans. It's time for me to remember."

"I know sweetheart" he assured her as he felt her relax against his chest. "Addie, you are so tired, please sleep, we can talk about it in the morning."

"I know but why, after all this time, it's been over two years, why can I remember it so clearly now?" She asked, raising her head to look him in the eye.

"God's time is not always our time, you know that Addie. You've said it so many times to me. It's all about the need to know, so maybe now you need to know."

"You're right again husband, God had to bless me with you first," Addie answered, relaxing against his chest, she fell asleep. Martin kissed the top of her head and held her until he was sure she was asleep, and then laid her down next to him. Martin lay beside her, praying for his wife.

CHAPTER 19

One by one they filed into the conference room; everyone was refreshed and ready to go. The table was set with enough breakfast to feed an entire army.

"I'll say one thing, Uncle Sam never fed us like this," Ray told Pike.

"Different enemy, different food," Pike answered.

When Addie walked in with Martin, every head turned.

"Hey Boss, better get some breakfast, Pike's out done himself," Dusty called out.

"I will, where's Wolff?" Addie asked, looking around the room.

"He hasn't come in yet," Holly answered.

"Snoop, where's Wolff?" Addie asked.

"Morning Boss, he's in the shower. You know Wolff he's on Wolff time."

Addie smiled and took her chair; Pike brought her breakfast. She'd been through this before; special job, special food. Good thing she liked all the food she was allowed to eat. As she poured the packet of orange powder laid out for her into her water, she saw Nick and Lilly coming into the room. Nick spotted Martin right away, his eyes lit up when he saw the sweet roll Martin had just put on his plate.

"Hi Addie," Nick waved. Taking Lilly by the hand, he pulled her toward the food.

"Those two are so cute. Eat up Addie girl, I made yours and Wolff's myself," Pike said, sitting a plate down in front of Addie.

All eyes turned when they heard Wolff's voice from the door. "I sure hope it's better than the crap you fed me last night," Wolff said, walking over to stand in front of Addie.

"So, does that mean you've decided to stay?" Addie asked.

"Yeah, when have you ever known me to leave you when you needed me?"

"Paris," Addie answered. She heard both Ray and Dusty cough.

"I did not I knew you could handle the rest of the assignment. Besides, I didn't leave, ask Snoop."

"He's right," They all heard Snoop's voice coming through the speakers. "Wolff was always within eyesight of you, always watching until you boarded the plane home."

"Now you see us, now you don't," Jacob added.

Wolff nodded and took his place at the table as Pike put a plate down in front of him. "I don't care what else you eat, but drink the orange stuff and eat this before you eat anything else," Pike instructed. Wolff looked over at Addie who smiled back and nodded.

"Holly," Addie called out, "when you are finished, you and Snoop can start the status update."

"Ready now Boss," Holly answered. She picked up her pad and a remote from a table in the front of the room. When she pressed the remote, wooden panels on the wall opened, revealing a screen that covered the center section with smaller screens all around it. When she pressed another button, the big screen moved forward and came to life.

"It's all yours, Snoop," Holly said.

What they saw next was a grid with icons of three planes flying cross country from the US to Panama City. "This was last week, before we all arrived. They took off right after those bastards and made me blow up my shop."

"Snoop, the children," They heard his wife say in the background.

"Sorry, I forget we have junior partners on this one," Everyone looked over at them; Nick just kept eating and Lilly blushed slightly. "Anyway, they landed and set up shop watching our office in Panama City. From what I can tell they didn't see you all go in or out."

"What makes you so sure?" Wolff asked.

"When they reported back to Henry, they confirmed they were in position and there had been no activity spotted at our headquarters."

"You got a live feed to Henry? How did you manage that?" Jacob asked.

"Not to Henry, that is unless he speaks, but I got ears all around the forward-looking team."

"Were you able to locate where Henry is? Is he still in the states?" Wolff pressed.

"He was, but now he's on the way headed your direction. I can't tell yet where he will land yet, but he's defiantly getting closer."

"Wonderful, or should I say the game is afoot," Angus said enthusiastically.

"More like, let the games begin," said Bird.

"I like games," Bat added.

"So, where are the forward-looking ones hanging out when they aren't on the job watching headquarters?" Wolff asked.

"Several different Hotels around our block, but so far I haven't located a headquarters where they all get together. Maybe when Henry arrives."

"No, he'll keep them spread out like sleeper cells. He's already given them their assignments. As soon as they figure out whatever trigger he gave them, like identifying one of us, they'll carry out their assignment," Addie told them.

"You know this how?" Ray asked.

"Because that's the way we'd do it," Wolff answered. "Henry's following the same pattern."

"I agree," seconded Jacob.

"So, Boss, give the word," Dusty said.

Addie looked over at Wolff. "What do you think, partner?"

"Snoop do we know how the teams are set up?" Asked Wolff.

"We do, in three's. There are twelve men in all. I got one team set on the roof tops of the block surrounding Solomon Inc., and one team on the ground watching the block on foot. From what I've noticed, they trade off with the other two teams around 10:00 p.m. Guys, these boys are just like the last ones," Snoop answered.

"How so?" Asked Bat.

"All young, trained, but not extensively, no family to speak of or to come looking, including dear old Uncle Sam."

"AWOL or dishonorable?" Asked Ray.

"All dishonorable and looking for work and all former deep and I do mean deep black project minions," answered Snoop.

"What are you thinking, Ray?" Addie asked.

"I'm thinking we take out his team. So, when he gets here, he will only have whoever is with him in the plane."

"Pick your team," said Addie.

"Jacob, Dusty, Austin and I will take care of the day shift. Pike, can you, Bird, and Bat take care of the night shift?"

"Be careful, this is way too easy and it might be a trap. There might be others hidden, just waiting for you to start taking out these boys. The ones we know about might be bait to draw us out in the open," Addie warned.

"More like to split the team, so that we aren't here to help you. Maybe we should just sit tight," said Ray.

"Tan and I will be here with Addie. The rest of you get in and get this thing done, and don't lose anyone, got it?" Wolff said.

"We all got it," Bird answered.

"Hey, what about the rest of us, Addie?" Nick asked, looking over at Addie.

"Nick, I need you, Tan, Wolff and Martin here helping me get ready for round two in this fight," Addie explained.

"What about Lilly?" Asked Nick.

143

"I need Lilly, Debbie, and Angus to help me with the documents we found at Headquarters. We need to piece together this puzzle so we know what we're up against," Holly told him.

"Well, just so I can use my training. You know, Tan didn't train me to come sit around and watch all of you, right Tan?" Nick asked.

"Yes, but remember rule number two," Tan reminded him.

"Yeah, rule number two, do what the Boss tells me to do and do not ask questions," Nick recited.

It took a minute before anyone could say anything they were all fighting to keep from laughing.

"Let's get this done," Ray called out. "Snoop, get us everything you have on the position of the players. Jacob, do you know where Trask kept his toys?"

"On it, I'll send it to your phones," Snoop replied.

"Follow me, your all going to love Trask's toy room," Jacob said, heading for the door with the rest of the team following behind.

"What's next Boss?" Tan asked.

"Holly, take your team and let me know as soon as you have anything. The rest of us are going to start working on the portal," Answered Addie. She was heading for the door with her team close behind, leaving Holly, Debbie, Angus and Lilly alone in the conference room.

"Did she say Portal?" Holly asked, looking over at Angus.

"She did, but trust me, you don't want to know," Debbie answered, before Angus could.

Holly shook her head and motioned to a door at the other end of the room. "Well then, we better get to work, the back hallway leads to the library, I had all the boxes delivered there," Holly led the way. Debbie noticed that Lilly wasn't following them and she had a strange look on her face, like she was looking at something or someone standing in front of her. Debbie walked over and bent down so they could talk face to face. Holly and Angus stopped at the door and waited, once they noticed they weren't following.

"What is it Lilly? Do you see something?" Debbie asked.

"No, I don't see anything," Lilly answered. Debbie noticed that she didn't look at her when she spoke. She took Lilly's hand and realized that the little girl was cold and shaking.

"Don't be scared, I'm here and I won't let anything hurt you," Debbie told her. Holding tight to her hand, they started to follow Holly out of the room when Lilly said, "Wait," Letting go of Debbie's hand, she ran to the nearest table and grabbed a salt shaker. Quickly screwing off the lid, she put some in her palm and ran back to Debbie. She almost ran into Debbie as she looked back.

When she got to Debbie, she turned and threw the salt back at the place she'd come from, then ran toward the door, stopping to pour more salt on the floor in the doorway. Looking up, she smiled and motioned for Holly, Angus, and Debbie to come through the door. Angus smiled knowingly as he joined the ladies.

She didn't say anything she just stayed between them holding their hands. When they reached the library, the door was ajar. Lilly let go of their hands and ran to the door. She looked down at the floor, salt shaker in hand, then turned back at them smiling. Angus stepped forward and opened the library door and motioned for the ladies to follow.

"Yes child, that's plenty of salt, you won't need the shaker. Put the lid back on so we don't make a mess, come on," he said. He took Lilly's hand and led her toward a long table with boxes stacked on top. "Let's get started, we have lots of work to do."

"Doesn't Addie need your help with the portal?" Debbie asked, with Angus following.

"Not yet, not until I see more of what we have here. I laid the plans for the portal out on the table in the lab. Between Addie and the men she has with her, they will have no problem setting things up," Angus answered.

"Setting what up?" Debbie pushed.

"That's what I hope all of this will tell us," Angus answered, pointing at the boxes piled up on library table.

"Tell me child, why were you spreading salt this morning?" Angus asked. He walked over to Lilly, who was looking at some documents on the table. She moved the documents around and stood back looking at them, as though she had been given instructions. She walked back, moved them around on the table again, and then looked to her side and smiled, like someone was standing there.

"Lilly, the salt?" Angus pressed again.

"Oh, sorry, he told me to throw it at the shadow and put it by the door. He said that way the shadow could not get out and follow us."

"Did you see anyone in the room with us?" Holly whispered to Debbie. Debbie just shook her head.

Angus acted like it was a normal thing, and he put more papers in front of Lilly. "Lilly, the person who told you that, did they tell you what their name was?"

"Sure, he did," Lilly answered. Pulling at his coat, he bent down to let her whisper something in his ear.

"Extraordinary! Tell me, is he still here?"

"Yes, he's right there, and Angus?"

"Yes child."

"Not these papers, the ones we want next are in that box over there. These will come later," Lilly answered, pushing the pile aside.

"Did he tell you that?" Angus asked. He grabbed the box she pointed at, and they all watched as she pulled out the papers, looked at them and nodded, then arranged them the way she wanted. Debbie looked over at Holly who shrugged her shoulders and walked to the table to watch Lilly.

146

Debbie came closer to Angus and asked, "What's going on?" Angus leaned in and whispered as they watched Holly helping Lilly with the papers. "This is extraordinary? My dear Ms. Debbie, he's helping."

"Who's helping her and what's he helping her with?"

"King Solomon, he's here in this room and he's helping her reassemble his testament."

"Lilly is talking to King Solomon? How do you know it's Solomon? You believe his testament is real?"

"Who else would know how the pages go together? And yes, I personally do believe it's real, even though most religious circles don't."

"So, how can that help us now?"

Angus looked at her like she should have not only known, but been excited about it. "Ms. Debbie, have you not been listening at all? We're not only fighting a physical foe, we're fighting an unseen foe. Possibly some of the worst hell has to offer."

"And we need his testament to win," Lilly said, stopping her work. Holly looked over at Debbie and Angus and shrugged. Debbie sighed and followed Angus to the table.

"Of course, we do my dear, well put, very well put," Angus said, patting her on the shoulder as one by one they took turns handing her the boxes she asked for.

When she'd finished she stopped, patted the stack of papers, and started twirling around the room like she was dancing to only music she and her invisible partner could hear, singing. "To God be the Victory."

"Oh my," Angus said smiling.

"What?" Debbie and Holly both asked at the same time.

"King David must be here too, that was his battle cry and he loved to dance," Angus answered like he was talking about an old friend.

They watched as Lilly came to a stop back in front of the table, bowed to her partner, and then walked to the pile of papers. As they watched, she picked up one of the boxes that was now empty and put the papers inside. Lilly appeared to be following someone. Angus motioned for them to follow, but not to interfere.

"Where do you think he's leading her?" Debbie asked Angus.

"My guess is to the chamber Addie must be ready for the documents."

CHAPTER 20

"Snoop, what's the plan to get us in?" Ray asked.

"That's my job," Jacob answered.

"Lead on," Ray said, looking over at Pike.

"He knows the layout, he helped Trask design a tunnel system that leads in from three blocks away," Pike told them.

"It was part of some kind of water system," Jacob answered, looking over at Bird and Bat.

"You want me to be a sewer rat?" Dusty asked, "Better not be any of those big ass spiders down there, you know how I hate."

"Relax its dry and we have a man that keeps it clean in return for having a place down there," Jacob answered.

"Great," said Bird.

Ray followed Jacob as he approached what looked like an old warehouse. The door opened as they pulled up. Once both SUV's were in, the door closed behind them. Following Jacob's lead, they parked, got out, and started to unload the weapons.

Ray grabbed for the last gun. Throwing it over his shoulder, he turned to join the rest of the group. When he turned away from the back of the SUV, he came face to face with a well-built man in cameo with face paint, that looked to be maybe fifty and crazy. He was holding a very impressive gun on Ray.

"Manuel, at ease, these are friends," Jacob said. Coming close, he put his hand on the end of Manuel's gun barrel and pushed it down.

"Jacob, welcome I didn't see you. Is the end upon us? Is this the final battle?" Manuel said with excitement in his voice.

"I hope not old friend, but I'm afraid it's started."

"That's what God has been saving this old rat for. What's the plan Jacob?"

"Snoop, you got our people in place? You got a strike plan?"

"You want me to help you shoot?" Manuel asked.

"Sorry, not this time Manuel. How about you help me with a diversion and some clean up?" Jacob asked.

"I can do that. Follow me."

"Snoop, you got a plan?" Jacob pressed.

"Yeah, give the old rat an ear piece," Snoop answered.

Manuel put the piece in his ear and grimaced, he hated hearing voices in his ear when he couldn't see who was talking.

"Manuel take Bat, she's the lady of the group, to the bakery. She can do the hit on the man having coffee. Take Jacob to the art gallery, I want him to take out the man on Solomon's rooftop. Take Pike to the tailor's shop, I want him to take out the man on the opposite rooftop. Then turn Ray and dusty loose on the ground in the alley to get the other two on foot.

"You're missing one man there should be another one up top, right? Three in the air and three on the ground," Jacob pressed.

"Yeah, I just can't find him. Get in position, I'll keep looking," answered Snoop.

"Not good enough man, we need to know," growled Jacob.

"You will, just give me a ... there we go. He's in the alley behind Solomon, in the courtyard. Ray, either you or Dusty can have him."

"You want any alive?" Jacob asked Ray.

"No. Judging from what we've been seeing, none of them would know anything. They probably don't even know that Henry is on his way. We take them out and clean them up, then regroup and go after the night shift. That is, if Snoop can find them by the time we finish," Ray said.

"I'll have a location long before you are finished with these boys. Remember, you guys are getting old," said Snoop.

"Yeah-yeah, just get us that location. I want to hit them long before they get up for a shift change," Ray told him.

"You got it Boss."

Some of the shop keepers were positioned at opposite ends of the block, setting up road cones with bright colored signs of a pending block party that night. One by one, Manuel led the operatives to their target locations. He then circled back, to let them back into the tunnel and assisted them in bringing the bodies back into the tunnel. He waited for the snipers to return, then went up top to help carry down the bodies.

"Snoop, all accounted for, you got the sleeper location?" Ray asked.

"Of course, I do, I got them four blocks away in a small house. I count six bodies, which should be all of them. How do you want this to go down?"

"We'll park around the area, about a block or so away. Bird, you and Bat think you can play the love struck kissy-face couple out for a walk?" Asked Ray.

"We sure can," Bird answered. He looked over at Bat who grinned and nodded back.

"While their distracting out front, Manuel, can you make a small disturbance in the back yard? Nothing big, just a little boom," Ray cautioned.

"No problem Boss, just a little boom."

"What about us?" Jacob said, pointing back and forth between himself and Dusty.

"Dusty, you keep an eye out for any stragglers. Jacob, Pike, and I will take the house. Any questions?" Asked Ray.

Everyone shook their heads and headed back down the tunnel to their cars. Manuel grabbed a duffel bag from a workbench in the warehouse before climbing in beside Dusty.

"What's in the bag man?" Dusty asked Manuel.

"What the Boss wanted."

"You mean a?"

"Yeah, a little boom."

"Great, just make sure it doesn't go boom in my car, got it?" Dusty told him.

"You worried about your car man? It's sitting on my lap, with way more important stuff than your car," Manuel reminded him.

Dusty rolled his eyes and followed Snoops coordinates to his position. Once he stopped, Manuel was out of the car and gone. Dusty settled in to watch the show, wishing he had some popcorn.

"And…action," he heard Snoop say through his ear bud.

As he watched, Bird and Bat strolled down the street. Bird was feeling her up, pulling her close, as she snuggled in and kissed his neck. They started kissing as they came to a stop in front of the house.

Kissing her hard, Bird leaned Bat up against the brick wall in front of the house, right in full view of a camera, gun in hand, hidden by Bat's body. It didn't take long for one of the men to come out of the house toward them. Bird shifted Bat in his arms and dropped him before he left the porch. As they headed down the street, they heard the small explosion behind the house followed by several pops from inside the house.

Bird and Bat waited back at their car for directions. When Ray and Jacob got back, Ray's instructions were for Bird and Jacob to scope out Henry's arrival. The rest of the team would return to the compound.

Less than ten minutes after they arrived, they were back on the road. Dusty dropped Manuel off at the warehouse before heading out of town.

"Man, you need help with all those bodies in the tunnel before I head back?" Dusty asked.

"No my friend, I have plenty of help and plenty of time, be well. When this is over, come by before you head out. You and I will share a drink and maybe I can scare up a woman or two, no?" Manuel told him.

"Only one or two? You got it man, you know I will if the Boss let's me," Dusty answered and then took off.

Snoop gave everyone coordinates, sending them back to the compound in different directions than any of them had come in.

Bat looked over at Pike, "Never go back the same way you came."

"That's the rule," said Bat, smiling. She slid down in the seat and laid her head back, feeling suddenly exhausted.

CHAPTER 21

Jacob and Bird waited for Snoop to come up with something.

"Snoop, you got anything? There's only a couple of places close enough to the city for him to land a plane that size," Jacob pressed.

"What's your hurry, you got someplace better to go?"

"I always got someplace better to go. It's you that never crawls out of whatever hole you're in."

"How wrong you are my friend, you just don't know it."

"Guys, can we get on with this? Snoop, you have to have eyes on Henry by now, don't you?" Bird pushed.

"I do, what I'm looking for is cover for you two. This place is out in the wide open."

"Put though the coordinates and let us worry about the cover," Jacob told him. A few seconds later, the SUV's screen lit up. Jacob looked at the map, hit the steering wheel, and they were gone.

"I take it you know this place? Is it a hard place to conceal?" Bird asked.

"I do and Snoop is right, then again I wouldn't expect any less from Henry. He knows we're here, he just doesn't know where. One thing I know about Henry, he plays to win," answered Jacob, looking straight ahead.

"You got a plan?" Asked Bird.

"Hey Snoop, you know how many we have in the air and on the ground?"

"Four in the air, at least six on the ground and two SUV's, the SUV's are Government issue, so I don't think what you brought will put a dent in them."

"I got some fun stuff with me," Bird said. Jacob looked over at his partner.

"Man, you're almost as bad as Wolff. Do tell, what's in the trunk?"

154

"Not in the trunk," Bird said, throwing a shiny object up in the air. Jacob turned to see and caught it, holding it up for him.

"Damn Bird man, where'd you get that?"

"This, my friend, is one of Manuel's special loads and I got six."

"Manuel says it will pierce the armor on these SUV's?" Jacob asked.

"Manuel says it will go through three layers and still leave one hell of a hole when it comes out the other side."

"Bird, you better hope Manuel isn't yanking your chain on this one," said Jacob, shaking his head.

"Never known him to be wrong yet, have you?" Bird asked.

"No, but I sure as hell don't want this to be the first time. You got any Intel or phone sync inside the SUV?" Jacob pressed Snoop.

"Sorry man, all black and all blocked," Snoop answered.

"What about ways out? I remember two, is that right?" Jacob asked.

"Yeah, two ways, but if they head back to the city there's only one."

"Then they'll take the other way," Bird told them. Jacob looked over at Bird.

"You don't think they'll touch base with the men in the city?" Jacob asked.

"I wouldn't, Henry can direct them from anywhere or send whoever he has with him to do it. He's headed to a safe house, and I'd say it's somewhere high so he can take off if he needs to. Snoop, run all the data, he's still on the payroll at NSA and CIA, someone has to have a place around here that's good enough to accommodate Henry's needs."

"On it, let you know as soon as I have something."

"Snoop, make it fast, I want to take out anyone I can as fast as I can," Bird told him.

155

"You got it."

Jacob pulled over to the side of the road into some trees as Bird looked down at the screen. They were less than a quarter of a mile from the runway, which was nowhere in sight.

"You got a plan?" Bird asked.

"No, how about you?" Jacob asked.

"Snoop, check the aerial view, we got anything on the ground we can blow up?" Asked Bird.

"Airplane fuel, guys think fast they're about to land."

Both men pulled their guns. Bird put the three bullets from Manuel in his pocket and buttoned them down, while handing the other three to Jacob. They looked at each other and smiled.

"Jacob, do you remember that time in East Berlin?" Bird asked. They went around to the back of the SUV, pulling out the duffel bags and rifle cases.

"Yeah, but we had more cover and it was dark."

"Minor details, you got your rifle? Jenny, is it? We got jet fuel, what more do we need?"

"A place to shoot from would be nice, some C4, it could be dusk."

"Getting soft man, where's the fun if it's all easy?"

"I like easy and I like my fun soft, curvy and warm, telling me not to stop."

Bird smiled back as they headed out through the trees toward the landing strip. By the time they reached the area, Snoop was giving them Intel through their ear buds. They split up to make it look like the airfield was surrounded.

The first shot fired was one of Manuel special rounds. They watched the last barrel in line, as one by one they blew. Bird smiled thinking Manuel hadn't lied. The two men watched as everyone scattered to ready position, moving toward the SUV's. There was still no sign of Henry.

Now it was Jacobs turn. He ran from the other side of the runway to the back of the plane. He fired one of

156

Manuel's specials straight into the fuel tank, just as the last of the passengers were on the tarmac walking away from the plane. One of them was Henry, and one other. Since there were only two of them, they decided to let everyone leave and they would follow. As they watched from the trees, Henry left in one SUV three others left with him. Four were left behind to clean up.

Jacob dropped the first one. When the other three turned his way, Bird took out the next one. The third turned and fired a rapid round in his direction Bird thought he was a dead man but from the corner of his eye he thought he saw a light and then felt a push, he stumbled just in time but damn if one didn't hit the side of his leg. Without moving, gritting his teeth and mad as hell, Bird took the last two out without giving Jacob a chance.

"Hey man," he heard in his ear bud, "the last one was mine."

"Sorry, number three made me mad when he shot me," Bird answered.

"How bad? Can you make it back to the truck?" Jacob asked, on the move to the hidden SUV.

"Meet you there," Bird answered, tying off his leg. He was up and on the move.

Jacob exchanged the first aid kit for Bird's riffle, shaking his head and smiling.

"Don't say a word man, not a word," Bird warned. He held up his hand, trying not to limp, as he quickly moved to get in.

"How bad is it man?" Jacob asked.

"Bad enough to need stitches and alcohol."

"Clean, or is the bullet still in you? And there won't be any alcohol until..."

"Clean, keep on them, I don't want to lose them. We need to get a fix on a location for them."

"Sure, how long can you last? How bad are you bleeding?"

"Just don't lose them, don't worry about me," Bird told him.

"Dude, don't flatter yourself, it's not you I'm worried about, it's me. If you die and I have to tell Bat, don't get me wrong she is beautiful, but she can be mean as hell."

"I'll try not to die. I'd hate for her to torture you," Bird answered.

"Here we are the evil lair. I can't believe the old man is slumming it. Snoop, you got a fix on this place?" Asked Jacob.

"Fix and eyes, think you can tag their rides before you head back in?" Snoop teased.

"I can, how about you Bird man?" Jacob asked, looking over at Bird when he didn't answer.

Bird was slumped against the passenger door.

"Damn it Bird," Jacob said, grabbing for his throat. There was a pulse, but it was week. Jacob didn't wait or check any further, he turned in his seat to grab his duffle bag and gun. He was out of the car and back in less than five minutes. He climbed in, buckled up, and they were off.

"Snoop, you got a signal on them?" Jacob asked, driving as fast as he could.

"I do, thanks," Snoop answered.

"Good, now get me to the nearest Solomon doctor, Bird is down. Make sure wherever you send us has blood, he's..."

"He's *A positive*. GPS is up, follow it, they'll be waiting for you. Jacob, how bad is Bird?"

"Don't order any flowers yet, Bird is one of the biggest bad-asses I know. How far until..."

"Ten more miles, tops. Man, you better hope he's a bad-ass because if he dies, there isn't a place on the earth you can hide from Bat and Addie," Snoop reminded him.

"I'll take care of Bird, you keep an eye on Henry," Jacob told him. He pulled up to the back of a warehouse, the loading dock door opened and he drove in. Before he could get out, they were pulling Bird out of the SUV. His head fell back as they lifted him to the gurney. They were off and running by the time Jacob got out. A young woman was handing him a cup of coffee, leading him away from the SUV and showing him where he could clean up and get something to eat.

Jacob called Addie; he didn't know who he should fear more, Addie or Henry. When he hung up he rubbed his forehead and asked the young lady if she had anything stronger than coffee. He had his orders, as soon as he got some sleep and knew how Bird was, he'd be moving in on Henry. The team needed to know any and everything they could about Henry and his team's movements.

Jacob jolted awake, grabbing for the young lady's hand as she gently shook him. He stopped short of hitting her, still holding tight to her wrist. Seeing the look of concern on her face, but thankfully not fear, he quickly let go.

"I'm sorry, I tend to come out fighting, I guess I'm just not use to having a beautiful woman wake me up. God, I hope I didn't hurt you, I mean your wrist," Jacob said, noticing that she was rubbing her wrist.

She smiled back at him and let her hands fall to her sides.

"Sir, it's alright, you didn't hurt me, maybe just a bruise or two."

Jacob hung his head, "It's not Sir, not anymore, just Jacob. I feel really bad."

"Okay Jacob, I'm Julie. What do you say we go see your friend and if you really feel bad, you can buy me dinner?"

Jacob looked over at her, smiled and nodded. He followed her into a make shift hospital room. Bird lay on the bed motionless; it was hard to tell who was whiter, the sheets or him.

"Dr. this is our patients associate, Jacob," Julie told the doctor.

"How is he?" Jacob asked.

159

"Stable, and that's all I can say for now. He lost a tremendous amount of blood. We removed two bullets, but they did a lot of damage. I have orders to move him back to the compound as soon as he's stable. I'll go with him, and he will make a full recovery," The doctor explained.

"Thanks Doc, I'll see you later. Please don't let him die, he's one of the very few friends I have left," Jacob told him.

"Well son, you can always get another friend, but if I lose one of Addie's men, there's no place I can hide."

Jacob nodded at the doctor, knowing exactly what he meant. As he passed Julie at the door to the room, he leaned over and whispered in her ear, "I'll be back, and you and I will have dinner and desert," She turned her head and kissed his cheek.

"Maybe we should have desert first," She answered, and turned to walk back into the room. Jacob smiled as he walked out.

"Snoop, you got coordinates?" Jacob said, tapping his ear bud.

"Hey man, you can whisper and I can still hear you, quit with the tapping. The car is fully loaded with coordinates, ammo, fire power and speed. Everything is just the way you like it."

"Great, let Addie know, later man," Jacob answered.

"Jacob, where you headed?" Snoop asked.

"To hurt Henry and anyone with him, now it's personal," answered Jacob. He pulled away from the warehouse and headed back to the edge of the city to get a new partner.

"You think Addie will approve?" Snoop asked.

"Just tell her this one's on me. Hey Snoop, tell Manuel to be ready, I'm coming to pick him up."

"Did you say Manuel?" Snoop pressed, "Are you sure? He's, well, kind of unstable."

"That makes two of us. Just tell him to be ready," Jacob said.

"Fire power?" Asked Snoop.

"Anything he wants to bring," said Jacob.

"Man, you're scaring me. He'll be ready."

CHAPTER 22

"Sir, we're ready to move whenever you are," the young operative said.

"We move out in ten minutes," Henry answered, turning his back to the young man.

When Henry heard the door shut, he turned back and began pacing around the room. He was going through each move of his plan over and over in his head. Damn Addie and her whole team. He'd trained them all and now he was going to have to kill each and every one of them. What a shame, there are only so many of them here at this time in history and they really were the best of the best.

Then again that made killing her team, one by one, in front of her, especially Wolff, even more appealing to him. Then and only then would he kill Addie, and he'd take his time with her. He had several new toys and medications he'd wanted to try out. After all, it was because of Addie and her team that he'd had to shoot his wife that is earlier than he'd planned to. It was inevitable, but he had planned on keeping her around a little longer.

"Sir, the car is ready for you," the young man said.

Henry nodded, picked up his gun from the desk, and followed the young man out to the car.

Jacob pulled up to the warehouse door, which immediately opened for him. He drove in and the door closed behind him. Manual was standing next to one of his work benches, loading a duffle. As Jacob approached, he turned a block of C4 in his hand. He waved, letting Jacob see what it was, before dropping it into the duffle.

"Man, you scare the hell out of me. You get what I asked for?" Jacob asked.

Manual just pointed toward the other end of the bench. Jacob walked over and unzipped the case. He looked down at the rifle and scope; reaching down softly, he ran his fingers along the length of the gun like it was a woman's leg, sighing as he did. He said softly, "Baby, you are so beautiful."

"Soft, always there for you and always deadly, I know what you mean man, just like a woman," Manual said, pointing to the SUV on the other side of Jacob's.

"Manual, if your women are like this rifle, all I got to say is we need to find you some new women," Jacob closed the case and headed for Manual's SUV.

"You can tell me the plan on the way," Manual said, climbing in the driver side.

"Snoop dog, you got a trail?" Jacob asked. Smiling, he threw Manual an ear bud.

"Hey," they heard Snoop say, "who you calling a dog, you old mutt."

Manual smiled over at Jacob and fired up the engine. They were on the hunt this time and they would not come home empty handed.

CHAPTER 23

Lilly led the way, appearing to be listening intently to someone, showing no signs of fear. They followed her into the elevator and down to the fourth level and down the hall. Angus smiled, knowing she was one of them.

At the door to the chamber room, Angus stepped forward to scan his eye. The door opened and Angus stood back, allowing Lilly to follow her friend into the room. As they watched, Lilly walked over to the table and set down the box. Together they all walked to the opposite side of the room where Addie, Wolff, Martin, and Pike stood in the circle of Solomon that was imbedded in the floor. They all stood looking at the half circle that was made by the clocks in front of them.

Lilly walked straight to them and said. "Addie, your key fits the clock in the middle, and it has to be wound. The King says he'll show me how to do it. He says his ring was first given to a child, and he will show me where it is, so that I can give it to you. Should I listen to him?"

Addie looked up to see King Solomon standing beside Lilly.

"Yes, he will lead you, here's the key, do what he says," Addie instructed. She took the chain from around her neck and handed it to Lilly.

Lilly looked to her side and smiled as they all watched, she put out her hand like she was holding someone else's and walked toward the clock in the center. As she reached the clock, she stopped and straightened her body. When she did, Lilly was lifted until she was even with the face of the clock.

She reached out, opened the glass door, and immediately placed the key in the round hole under the hands. As she turned it slowly, she recited some words Addie knew were Aramaic, but could not translate.

Instinctively, she looked over at Angus who was recording every word.

When Lilly had completed the rotation of the wind, everyone heard a chime from inside the clock and watched as Lilly floated back down to the floor. She nodded once again and reached out to touch a wooden panel on the front of the clock, and pushed it. When she did, the wood creaked and the panel opened, reveling the weights and balances of the clocks inner workings.

They all stepped forward to see Lilly reach for one of the weights in the shape of a pine cone. Lilly took it in her hand and turned it over, revealing a small latch. She opened the latch allowing the two halves of the weight to separate. What they saw nestled in the middle of the weight surrounded in deep purple cloth was a ring. Without hesitation, Lilly took the ring. Holding it in her hand, she titled her head to listen, then closed the case, replaced the weight, and softly shut the door to the clock. She turned and walked straight to Addie.

Addie heard Solomon say, "Kneel down woman, and accept the wisdom and dominion of God from this innocent hand," Addie immediately did what she was told, as Lilly recited again in Aramaic. When she was done, out of nowhere, Addie could feel and smell sweet oil running over her head and face. When she looked up, she saw them all: Solomon, David, Isaac, Trask, and Papa Time. They were all standing there smiling a faint glow of white outlined their bodies.

Solomon held the gold jar in his hand, which held the oil he had poured on her head. He held it up above his head, speaking in Aramaic he recited the same incantation as Lilly. When he finished, Solomon nodded at Lilly, who reached for Addie's right hand, placing the ring of Solomon on her signet finger.

Immediately a rush of current went through Addie. Her first thought was, *this must be what it feels like to be struck by lightning.* When she opened her eyes, she could not believe what she saw. All around her were demons on one side, and angels on the other, all were in a ready position. Behind Lilly, where the middle clock stood, was a door. Unable to stand, Addie could only watch as two huge angels with swords at their sides reached down and softly lifted her to her feet.

When she looked around the room, she saw Wolff on her right side and Lilly on her left. Everyone else in the room had formed a semicircle, and all were on bended knee. Addie tried to speak, but couldn't, until Solomon reached out and touched her lips with his finger and said. "Addington, tell them to stand and not to be afraid," Addie nodded, but first pushed the message back to him, "What about the evil ones?"

Solomon answered her question. "They are always all around us, every day this is their world until the second coming."

As he answered, one of them that appeared to be a leader stepped closer to them and hissed. "Take the ring back to where it came from. Stop this torment now, you have no right to control us, that is for the Son of God and it is not yet his time."

As he talked, Addie felt the ring on her finger start to tingle and heat. Looking down, she saw it had started to glow with a white light. She felt the angel on her right lift her arm, pointing it in the direction of the demon. As she did, the light could be seen to form a hologram of the Star of David. Addie noticed the invisible team had come to stand around her and the first line of angels had pulled their swords.

"The ring is where it will stay, on the anointed of God, until God himself tells her to return it. Remember, it is written that the children of God have dominion over all, including you and your legion of watchers until the end of time. Bow before the one that wears the ring and those she anoints"

With cursing, groans, and shrikes of pain, they all bowed.

"Addington, take this oil and put my star on both Wolff and Lilly's heads, then let the Holy Spirit have your tongue to bless them."

Addie did what she what she was told. The look on Wolff's face as he looked into her eyes to receive the blessing was that of amazement, tears rolled down his face. Lilly smiled up at her like she knew all along this was going to happen.

When Addie had finished, Solomon addressed the leader of the watchers who was allowed to stand.

"There is a human among you. I am allowed to call upon him and give him a choice to make. When I call his name, you will allow him to come forward in the name of the most high," Solomon commanded.

"He is mine! You have no right to take a departed soul who had time before he passed to make his choice," The demon cursed and spit at Solomon. Addie felt Wolff step forward and King David stop him, telling him that there will be a time to fight, but not now.

"As one who has dominion over you, I command you to turn him over or I will set loose the angel that frustrates you."

Again, the demon cursed and threatened Solomon. Solomon moved to stand directly in front of the creature as a huge angel, dressed in emerald green battle clothes, stepped out from the ranks and drew his sword, readying himself for battle and smiling.

The demon screamed for him not to touch him and Addie saw the look of terror on the demon's face.

"I call forth Jean Lafitte," Addie heard Solomon shout.

From the back of the legion of demons, Addie with Wolff at her side, watched as Jean Lafitte made his way through the pack until he was standing in front of Solomon. Immediately, he was forced down on bended knee.

"Who are you that summons me?" Lafitte choked out. "Are you God?"

"No, I am Solomon, God has given me charge over you. There is one among us who has commanded me to summon you."

Before Solomon had finished, Addie and Wolff saw the angels behind them bending down until they could see a man walking toward them. He walked softly, touching some of them as he walked past them. The glow from his touch was a beautiful deep purple and blue.

When he reached the first row of angles, Addie and Wolff felt themselves pulled to their knees. When the man got close enough, Wolff looked at his face, which was glowing with white light. Wolff felt sick, but then the light dimmed and he was able to look up into the man's face. Seeing it clearly now, he saw what melted the stone coldness of his heart. He saw the marks of the crown of thorns on the man's forehead. The man simply smiled back at Wolff as he walked on.

"Son of God, leave us, it is not your time. This is not your time we have more time than this. Bow down to me and join us and the world will be yours as it should have been," The demon hissed.

In a calm, authoritative voice he spoke, "It is written thou shall have no other God before me and that the Son of God will crush the head of the serpent and restore his kingdom in his time."

As Addie and Wolff watched, Jesus laid a pierced hand on Jean Lafitte's shoulder and asked him, "Jean, who will you follow, me?"

There was an awkward moment of silence before Jean spoke.

"Lord God, I will follow you."

The instant the words left his mouth, a deafening moan from the legion went up as they watched Lafitte be lifted to his feet into Jesus' embrace. Addie and Wolff watched as

Jesus lovingly hugged him. With his arm around his shoulder, side by side, Jesus and Lafitte walked back through the throng of angels who stood as they passed, blocking them from view.

When they were gone, the demon again cursed Solomon and asked why he had come and why the ring was once again on the hand of a human, a woman no less.

"First of all creature, you will show this woman respect and remember that it was God who chose a woman to bring his Son into the world. We have come to aid you and to command you concerning your duty at this time in creation."

"To aid us, how could you aid us?"

"There is one among the people of the earth who has attempted to duplicate the ring and writings. He wishes to control you for the purpose of controlling the wealth, properties, and dominion of the reigning governments and principalities. You know this will not be accomplished."

"He cannot control us, she wears the ring," the demon shouted.

"That is true, however, this man has been able to control a small number of your weakest ones through the ring he created and a portion of the writings he possesses," The demon whirled around, reaching down he grabbed for one next to him. Propelling him upward to face him, he began screaming into his twisted face.

"Who is this human, how do I not know about him, and who among us is he controlling? How did he discover that he had dominion? I will slaughter and send to the fire pit all who have joined with him," He screeched.

"Master, there were only a few I directed to follow him he is descended from one of us. He learned his control from the wretched woman who trained all of these people, but God showed her who he was and she refused to continue his training.

He stole some of her documents to study and found the way to contact us. He promised to seal the gate and to prolong the coming of the Son of God. I knew he couldn't, however, he provided us with a way to spread deception among their leaders. I gave him several followers to reek some havoc among the government. He promised to bring down Solomon Inc. God has plans for this company that we need to know. If we can slow down the transfer, we can martyr more humans worldwide," He pleaded as the life was being drained from him. His body was turned to dust, and the cries of his pain made Addie cover her ears.

The leader turned back to his legion and shouted, "Who do you all follow, decide."

The answer was unanimous, "You" all of them said, knowing that they were no match for him.

The leader turned back to Solomon with a look of defiance on his face. "He was a fool, as are those following your human. The plan is written in the scrolls and it will be carried out. I ask only that we have our allotted time and that you do not bind us. What deal do you offer us, King?"

"I have no deal, only this command, you will dispatch some to frustrate and kill all those under the command of the human, Henry Perrin. Either by your hand or by assisting the people of Solomon Inc., until he stands alone, you will then pull back your minions from around him and deal with them as you see fit."

"Will she kill this human and send him to me?" The demon demanded, pointing at Addie.

"This man will," Solomon assured him, pointing at Wolff.

"Then it is over? Will you take the ring and return it to heaven until the appointed day of the Son of God returns?"

"No, the ring will remain on Addie's finger, protected from all of your legions. She will not cause you harm or stop you from disturbing the humans, and in return you will assist her in transferring the wealth and power from the ungodly to the Elect," Solomon instructed him.

"How is that not interfering with us?" The demon shouted and moved closer to Solomon in a threatening way. As he did, the angel dressed in green stepped between Solomon and the demon, his sword now flaming, sending the demon shrinking back in horror.

"I never said I would not interfere with you, all humans have dominion over you and the ability to interfere with your plans. I said I would not bind or send you to the pit. You will be allowed to continue to walk the earth and take as many as you can until that day. By the power of the risen Lord of Hosts, I dispatch you to destroy those under the command of Henry Perrin and when Addie commands you, you will call back those that belong to you that surround him. When he falls, his soul is yours for eternity."

"From this day forth, Solomon Inc. will carry on the work allotted to them without your interference. When the wealth, power, and property are distributed by Solomon, completing God's plan, you know what happens then. Now, go forth and accomplish what you have been commanded."

Addie and Wolff watched as the legions who stood behind their leader with their heads still bowed, started to disappear before them. As they did, the air was lighter and it was easier to breath. The angles behind them rejoiced, and then they were gone. Solomon instructed Addie. "Addie, you and Wolff follow me, the battle is ours."

Addie nodded as Solomon pulled back, the room around them came back into view as Addie and Wolff looked around. Everyone was still on their knees praying being led by Angus.

"Tell them to stand Addie," Solomon instructed.

"Everyone, please stand," Addie said. Wolff walked over to each of the women, helping them stand. Holly and Debbie knew immediately there was something different in his touch. Wolff walked over to Lilly, picking her up he kissed her and put her on his back. Martin also noticed the difference in his demeanor. As he came close to Martin, he looked over and smiled at him.

"What happened Wolff, what did you see?" Martin asked.

"Martin, I had a come to Jesus," was all he said.

Martin smiled back, reached over to slap his shoulder, and simply answered, "Awesome."

As Martin turned back to his wife, he observed her talking to someone that he couldn't see. He stepped forward, hearing Addie ask, "Solomon, if the center clock held the key and the three together make the portal. What are the other keys for?"

Solomon simply smiled and reached out, putting a hand on her shoulder he said in a low voice, "All in due time, Addington. Take this bag, in it you will find pendants made of Agates and twisted wire. They were formed in the heavens, by the Father, the same as my ring. Each one designed to protect, instruct, or provide for the specific person it was made for.

Addie opened the bag and pulled one of the pendants out "There is no name on this one, who do I give it to?"

"Have your team form a circle you stand in the middle and one by one put one of the pendants in the palm of your hand. Repeat, pendant of God find your solider. An angel of the Lord will take it from your hand and deliver it to the proper person. They are not to take it off and are to wear it next to their skin."

"Why Agates, why the intricate wiring?" Addie asked.

"The Agate is a gem stone made by God, endowed with his peace and in his peace, is his greatest power available. The wire serves as a conductor; each one is different because each body conducts the spirit of God in a different way or path. Some more twisted than others," Solomon answered looking over at Wolff.

"I'll agree, I'm twisted," said Wolff

Solomon smiled, almost laughed, as he turned back to Addie. "Now go and finish the job for today."

I will return your key to God the Father until he instructs me to take back the ring. You and Wolff will keep the other two until the board reveals how to use them, and that's all I can tell you for now. Now, go, remember the victory is the Lords."

Addie nodded and turned back to see Martin and Wolff standing there watching her. "You two can talk later. Right now, we have finish this Wolff," Addie said, pulling Wolff toward the door.

"What do you need wife?" Martin asked.

"I need you to stay here and make sure Debbie, Holly and the kids are safe while Wolff and the rest of us finish this job."

"I don't like it, but I promised to listen to the boss," Martin answered, pulling her close and kissing her hard.

"Addie, the rest of the group is back, they're on the main floor. Do you want me to call them to the board room?" Asked Snoop.

"Yes," Addie said.

"Don't give us a second thought, we'll be here when you get back and until you do, we'll be praying," Debbie assured her. Addie nodded and gave her friend a hug. Addie and Wolff wasted no time heading to the board room.

"All hands on deck everyone. We don't have much time. Everyone form a circle around me."

They all knew the look on Addie's face. They gathered around, watching as one by one Addie pulled the pendants from the bag. They all watched in amazement as she recited what Solomon had instructed and saw the pendants being lifted by their chains, floating through the air to each person.

The first was Wolff, as the pendent got close to him Wolff instinctively lowered his head the chain was slipped over and dropped around his neck. Wolff looked at the beautiful stone wrapped in designs of wire and quickly dropped in inside his shirt next to his skin.

As he did he saw the deep amethyst light at his right side. As he watched a face appeared to form along with the body of a woman dressed for battle. She smiled at him, he turn back to see everyone in the circle looking at their right sides with a bewildered look.

"Addie I'm seeing something what's going on here?" Ray asked.

"Open your mouth and let the spirit speak," Solomon reminded Addie. Addie did as she was told and was surprised herself.

"Fear not, those who stand beside you are the guardians given to you at birth. They are yours and yours alone. Assigned to guard, protect and uplift you in times of need."

Wolff watched as the woman handed him a pouch. It was though time stood still. Hearing in his mind she instructed him to open the pouch. When he did, he found bullets of several sizes. He looked over at her bewildered and the answer came. Look at the writing on them. One by one he turned each one over and saw inscribed a city and a date. He looked over at the being once again and heard her say. "They were meant for you, I stopped them. It's part of my job."

Wolff was jolted from her as he heard Addie telling the group.

"Think of them as your good luck charm and your ear bud to heaven. They're meant for your protection and to allow you to see the other side when you need to," Addie instructed them. They all nodded and dropped them inside their shirts.

"Hey, what the hell," they heard Snoop say. "Addie I got one too," Addie smiled.

Snoop, you're up, talk to us," Addie said.

"Yeah well, we got Bird stable; he should make a full recovery." Snoop started to say, but was cut off by Bat.

"What? Stable? A full recovery from what, what the hell happened?" Bat demanded.

"Hold on girl, he just got shot a little in the leg. The problem is he lost a lot of blood before Jacob could get him some help, but all is well. He has a cute nurse fussing over him, so you know that will make him heal even faster," Snoop told them.

"Save it Snoop, where is he?" Bat demanded.

"Bat, you'll have to leave him in the nurse's hands right now, I need all of you with me. Snoop, where's Henry and his men?" Addie pressed.

"On their way to Solomon Inc., Panama's office."

"Where's Jacob, is he alone?" Addie asked.

"Jacob is at the art gallery with."

"With who?" Addie demanded. She was looking around the room thinking that they were all accounted for.

"With Miguel," Snoop answered hesitatingly.

"Miguel and Jacob are together? Please tell me there is no C4 anywhere close to Miguel," said Ray.

"I can't answer that man, Miguel keeps track of his own inventory," Snoop answered.

"Addie, we need to get there fast. With one of Jacobs friends hurt, him joining forces with Miguel and C4 is not a good mix," Pike chimed in.

"We need to get there fast before those two blow up the whole damn block," Wolff said.

"What's the plan, Boss?" Ray asked.

"Our enemy is Henry Perrin and whoever is working for him. Snoop, how many are we up against?"

"Less than six, Boss."

"We got eyes on the inside?" Ray asked.

"We did, but they got cut, shall we say. Henry is in the house," Snoop answered.

"Let's roll," Addie said. "I'll meet you all down stairs. Snoop, lock up behind us."

"Come home to me Addie, you know it's you and Wolff they're after," Martin told her. As he pulled her close, he felt her tremble. "None of that now, no fear, remember? Do whatever you have to, to end this. Solomon needs to get on with the business it was designed for."

"All this gushy stuff is making me sick," Nick said. Lilly leaned into him and took his hand. Nick looked over at her and saw that tears were rolling down her cheek. "Man, now see what you've done, you made Lilly cry."

Addie walked over to them. Bending down, she wiped away Lilly's tears and told them both not to worry, to mind everything Martin told them to do, and most of all they should pray. Lilly straightened up and looked past Addie and nodded.

"What is she looking at?" Nick asked.

"King Solomon is in the house," Addie told him. "What is he telling you Lilly?"

"It's not King Solomon, it's his father David. He says I am a princess and a child of the most high God, and that the victory is always the Lords. He said he killed Goliath with one stone and General Perrin won't even take a half a stone."

"Well if anyone knows battle it's David. As I recall, it's written that Saul killed thousands, but David killed tens-of-thousands," Angus recited.

"He told me the ladies were singing about that and he danced as the ladies sang. He said he kind of got into trouble, but he won't tell me how he got in trouble. Is that written down too?" Lilly asked.

"Come child, that's not important, Miss Debbie can explain that to you later. Addie, go in the Lord and be blessed, may the Lord deliver you from this battle," Angus said, making the sign of the cross on Addie's forehead with oil.

"Addie, the crew is ready, Bat, Pike, Tan, Ray and Dusty have already left, and Wolff is waiting for you. Jacob cleaned the roof man, you should have seen that shot, and he's placed a new camera up there. He's got several more on him and he's waiting for your orders to go in," Snoop told her.

CHAPTER 24

The elevator doors opened and Addie flew into the car and buckled up without saying a word. The smoke billowed from the tires as Wolff peeled out of the open door.

"Addie, I'm not trained for this and I never thought I would be asking you, but here we are, what do I do?" Wolff asked. He was speaking in his *in the zone* voice, which Addie had only heard from him a couple of times, the last of which was when they were in Paris.

The only thought that came to her mind was *Lord thank you for the privilege of having this man as my partner*. She was surprised to hear a response to her thank you.

"When the battle is won, make Wolff your full partner in Solomon Inc., but now tell him Perrin is his in the flesh. Those that surround Perrin will be destroyed and the man belongs to Wolff," Addie starred ahead, listening intently. Wolff noticed and knew better than to interrupt. When the full message had been given, Addie turned to Wolff.

Wolff, the training you'll need for today, you had already. The rest of the team will take care of Perrin's team. Solomon, David, and I will take care of those on the other side and Perrin will be left with only his human abilities, which should be an easy fight for you. That is unless you've gotten soft."

Wolff straightened up and looked over at Addie smiling. "Baby, you take care of those growling creatures we saw and leave Henry to me. I only have one question, does he live or does he die?"

"There are creatures waiting to escort him to his new headquarters. His position running project W.I.S.E will be terminated."

"That's all I need to know," Wolff answered.

"Snoop, is the block secured? No innocent bystanders going down today, you hear?" Addie warned.

178

"All clear and blocked off, I didn't even have to work on it, one of Perrin's boys did it for us. That man always was a stickler for details."

"Jacob, give us a rundown of positions," They heard Snoop's voice in their ear buds.

"Perrin had one man on the roof of Solomon Panama, and he's been neutralized. There are two with Henry inside, two wondering the block as look outs, and one in an SUV."

"I'm sure he's trying to listen," Addie added.

"He's trying to listen, but before I opened contact, I scrambled his receiver. All he's getting right now is white noise. I also cut all the cameras on the street they linked into."

"How does that help us with eyes on the street?" They all heard Ray ask.

"We have other camera's that don't show up on the grids in each one of the shops we own, I always have eyes on the street," Snoop told them.

"I love you man," Ray answered.

"You want me to go in and help the man in the van with his communication problems?" Miguel asked.

"Can you do it quietly without blowing anything up?" Asked Snoop.

"Sure, but it's not as much fun," Miguel answered.

"You can have more fun later. For now, wait for Jacob's signal until the other two on the ground are out of direct sight. Then, move in and take everybody in the van out, you got it?" Snoop asked.

"Sure, I got it," Miguel answered. He put on his straw hat and stepped out of the bakery, pastry in hand, and started to eat while walking slowly towards the van.

Wolff looked over at Addie. "Do your stuff baby, whatever that is."

Addie closed her eyes and spoke to the demons standing around the van on the street. Before she could say anything, she saw them kneel to the ground, their commander giving instructions.

"Leave the human and wait until his soul is delivered to you. Do not interfere with those who will send us his soul," Immediately, they stepped away from the young man on the street. As Addie and Wolff watched, two demons walked through the van walls to the street, waiting for more orders.

The creatures assigned to him did not have to wait long. As Miguel closed in on the van he finished the last bite of pastry and licked his fingers. He then pulled a knife from his belt and walked to the back of the van and tried the door, it was unlocked. The stupid kid hadn't even locked the door.

Miguel eased the door open and sprung at the young man inside, catching him completely off guard. He slit his throat and threw him to the floor of the van. As the young man bled out, Miguel destroyed everything in the van, but he didn't stop there, he planted some C4.

"Snoop, there's a cab on the street, how much time do I have? You should let me take it out, I don't want anyone missing all the fun," He asked.

"Enough, take out the cab."

Miguel exited the back and made his way to the cab. It was his lucky day none of the doors were locked. He crawled in, stomach on the seat, pulling every box and wire he encountered, and then smashed the starter and cut all the wires underneath. As he crawled out on the passenger side, he adjusted his straw hat and clothes and walked slowly back to the bakery.

As the young man in the van took his last breath, he saw the two hideous creatures coming for him. He screamed as their claws grabbed him, the pain was like hot pokers wherever they touched. Unimaginable pain shot through every fiber of his body. *What was happening,* he thought, as they pulled and scratched him? He looked back and saw himself laying there on the floor of the van, his throat cut, his eyes wide open, as the blackness closed in on him. He shouted "NO!" and heard them say.

"Welcome to your eternity. Pain, torture, and dark nothingness await you now and forever more."

As Jacob watched, the two men walking on the ground tried to contact the van to report an 'all clear' just as Jacob was being told that the other players were in position. When they couldn't make contact, they took cover. As they did, the demon protectors also pulled back, waiting to claim their prizes.

Tan took the one in the alley behind Solomon first. As he passed under the fire escape, Tan jumped down on him, snapping his neck as the demons stood back and cheered Tan on. Tan felt the pendant heat up, as it did he heard and saw the hideous creatures waiting to claim their prize. Tan had all he could do to collect himself and check in.

"I'm in position at the back of Solomon," Tan said. One by one the rest of the team, led by Ray, assembled, took cover, and resumed waiting.

"Snoop, I got guy number two," Pike said. "I can't let you boys have all the fun," The young man was still trying to contact the van, and passed by the tailor's shop at the end of the block. Pike stepped out of the open door and fired point-blank, hitting him right in the temple. His soul fell into the hands of his tormentors before his body hit the ground. Pike watched in amazement as the creatures dragged his soul away.

"Are we clear on the street?" Asked Snoop.

"All clear, heading to the team."

****

"Sir, there's nothing here. They must have found it already," The young solider said, seeing the anger rise in his commander's face. Henry turned, shot him, and shouted at

181

the other two, "Pull number five from the street and get him up here to help."

"Sir, yes Sir!" The young man answered, stepping over his fallen comrade. Little did he know; his friend's soul was being pulled away kicking and screaming in pain. A sudden shutter went through him. Unknown to him, a demon was whispering in his ear, "We'll have you next."

When he couldn't make contact, he hesitated to tell Perrin, after seeing what he'd just done, but he had no choice. As he turned to tell him, a shot from the doorway hit its mark and the young man dropped. Addie and Wolff stepped into the room with their guns drawn. At the sight of Addie and Wolff, the demons connected to Henry stepped away from his sides. Addie stood watching and smiling. Before words were exchanged, they heard another thud coming from the library.

"That was the last of them. Bat, you go girl, that was smooth," Snoops voice rang in their ear buds. "Don't miss the fun, they're in Trask's office."

Perrin smiled at Addie and Wolff, and walked to the bar to pour himself a drink.

"So, where do we go from here Addie?" Perrin asked, taking a long slow drink.

"We aren't going anywhere, but you're going to hell today," answered Addie.

Perrin laughed and drained the glass before he spoke, "I command hell, Addie girl, I found the secret. I recreated the ring of Solomon and I made a deal, step over and see," Perrin taunted.

"After you Henry. Step on over and see the deal I've made," countered Addie.

As they all watched, Perrin smiled and lifted his hand that was wearing the ring. As he did, he felt the sensation of water wash over him and the office faded away. Wolff and Addie watched as hordes of demons appeared around Henry. Addie and Wolff stood alone.

"You come alone you arrogant Bitch, you dare to think you alone can take me on?" Perrin spat at her.

"No, I'm leaving you for Wolff I promised him that he could kill you, you know, Paris, his sister."

"I see, so you're only here to watch?"

"No, I'm here to make it a fair fight and to see Wolff send you to hell. You know, an eye for an eye, for Isaac, Trask and Clair," Addie told him.

"Those morons and where are they now?"

"Right here, my darling husband," Claire's soft voice could be heard from the shadows as her spirit, dressed in glowing white, stepped forward. "I'm here to see you taken. You see, if you were to live, and you won't, it would have been to your surprise that none of my estate had been left to you or Ellis. It was all left to Solomon Inc."

Henry glared at her. "That's impossible, I saw the will."

"You and Ellis saw the will I wanted you to see. Not only is there another will there are documents of all the antics you and Ellis were up to. So, even if you would have lived through this, you and Ellis would have been in Prison for the rest of your lives."

"My dear, rest assured, I will live through this and you are simply not smart enough to pull something like that off," Henry said, taking a long drink.

"You underestimated your wife and your partners, Henry old friend. Did you really think we would let you kill us so easily? We all had to go, don't you see?" Trask's voice, strong and proud, came from the shadows as he and Isaac stepped out to stand by Clair.

"Here to watch you run the race, old boy, as it is written. Trask is right, we had to go to take our place on the board of directors running Solomon Inc. when we turn it over to Addie and Wolff. You, my friend, were always the short-sighted one," Isaac said.

They could see Henry flare with anger. He started to recite commands in a tongue that the demons seemed to

183

understand. As they started to move forward, he smiled at the thought of what he had instructed them to do to Addie.

Addie smiled back and stood her ground, she let them get close, but not too close. She waited until many of them had surrounded her before lifting her hand that wore the authentic ring of Solomon.

The creatures backed up, shrieking in pain. Perrin shouted commands and they moved in again to take her. Before any of them could lay a hand on her, the demons surrounding her backed away and screamed a horrific cry as the throng parted, they scrambled for cover, many of them were thrown around and kicked aside by two men accompanied by warrior angels. When they had made their way to Addie, they assembled behind her. As they did, the demons fell back, shrieking away from them.

"Who do you say you are? I order you by the name of the prince of the earth, tell me your names!" Perrin ordered.

The first man stepped forward wearing a sword at his side. "I am David, King of the Jews, who fights alongside the one you know as Wolff."

Perrin's color subdued and paled some.

"And I am Solomon, King of the Jews, son of David whose writings and the ring you seek to command. I will be the one to bind your army and turn your soul over to them when you are no longer in need of your body."

"I have made a deal and they are bound by the dominion I have over them to do my bidding," Perrin shouted at Solomon.

"Fool, have you not read what is written? The Son of God has come and crushed the head of these who you think follow you. While it is true you have dominion for a moment that is subject to one who can make a better deal. I am that someone and as is my right. I have given my authority to use my ring to this woman. Woman, command," Solomon instructed her.

Addie pointed the ring at Perrin and the throng behind him and called forth the commander of the legion. As they watched, the throng began to part and as the leader approached, they all dropped to their knees. A demon, most hideously dressed for battle, appeared and stood beside Perrin.

"Take her, I command you as one who has dominion over you," Perrin commanded the leader.

The demon looked at him and laughed. "Human, the woman commands the ring, the one from the hand of God. Simpleton, you do not see how my watchers deceived you," He bellowed at Perrin, pointing a bony finger at the ring on Addie's hand.

"Silence, you are mine to command," Perrin shouted.

"You be silent. Solomon, what is your business with this man?" The demon said, walking in front of Solomon.

"My job was to deliver the ring to the chosen of God and to keep him from deceiving you."

"Me? This stupid man did not deceive anyone in my army, but tell me, if he were to get the ring, what does heaven believe his plan was? The severity of his punishment is in the balance."

"He would have bound you all and made you slaves to him, not allowing you to walk free and wreak havoc. Your time is short enough before the King of Kings binds you, I would not let a human shorten my time."

"Don't listen to him, he's lying to you. My plan was always a partnership," Perrin interjected.

The demon turned to glare at him. "Fool, he can't lie, he is already redeemed on the other side. You on the other hand... Tell me, what is your bargain, King?"

"Command your legion to stand back and watch the fight between my warrior and the human. When this human is killed, you take his soul and go free, except for one thing."

"That is?"

185

"You and your kind will back away from all of the workings of Solomon Inc., and you will pay a tax to Solomon to be decided on by the board of directors. Take it from whatever human or government you like, and if you come across any operations of Solomon, you must depart and pull back your demons to allow Solomon to do their job."

"What a bargain, I pay and I pay again. What is in this for me, King?"

"You and your hoard will be allowed to go free. Solomon Inc. will not bind you until the day of days when the King of Kings binds you for the last time."

Without hesitation, the creature nodded and waved his hand. He turned his back on Solomon and as he walked to his legion, they all stepped back from Perrin. The Commander stopped in front of his army and folded his arms.

"It is a bargain, let the fight begin. We will stay and watch and collect our prize when it is done."

"No, No!" shouted Perrin. "We had a deal and I have dominion, I control you!" His words fell on deaf ears, no one paid any attention to Perrin. Those who watched faded from the room and once again they stood in the middle of Trask's office, surrounded by Addie's team. Perrin pointed his gun at Wolff. As he did, they watched as the gun appeared to be ripped from his hand.

"Now, now, fight fair Henry," Wolff said, moving forward. Henry dove at Wolff. The fight took a little longer than Wolff thought it would, but in the end, Perrin lay bloody and very dead on the floor before them.

As the cheers went up around the room, Jacob stepped forward to punch Wolff in the shoulder. The room turned ice cold and the smell of sulfur caused them all to gag. They all turned to see a swarm of demons taking a screaming Perrin as they pulled at his spirit with huge claws and sunk their teeth into him, causing him to writhe. He was unable to break free before he they disappeared into the shadows. They heard Perrin scream.

"There is another, there is another," Perrin screamed. Bat looked at Addie who shook her head.

Behind Addie, Bat could see David, Solomon, Trask, Isaac, and Papa Time, who was offering his arm to Clair. They Smiled back saluted all in the room as they disappeared into the mist. Addie looked around the room to see her team saluting back out of habit not believing what they had just witnessed, each person touching the pendant around their necks, shaking their heads.

CHAPTER 25

The next few months had been a whirlwind of activity. Wolff was appointed as the second senior partner, Ray was now a junior partner, and Jacob was now the head of the Panama office. Bird was fully recovered and he and Bat had disappeared for now, but would be back to work as the new operatives in charge of setting up additional divisions of Solomon throughout the world.

Nick and Lilly were reunited with their parents, who were happily married and living in Canada.

Holly had decided to take a couple of weeks off to visit Corey in New Orleans, leaving Snoop to hold down the fort. That suited him just fine, especially since a budding romance was in the air. The rest of the operatives returned to their locations with stories to tell that were out of this world.

Martin was glad to have his wife home for as much time as possible. Debbie and her husband, when he was not flying Addie around, were traveling and working with Angus and Pike to organize the paranormal jobs for Solomon Inc.

Wolff was on his way out when the wolf call sounded from his cell phone.

"Good morning partner, I was just on my way in."

"Meet me by the river this morning, will you Wolff?" Addie asked.

"Sure, do we have a problem?"

"No problem, it's time to discuss your training," Addie said and disconnected.

Wolff smiled and headed out.

DEDICATIONS

To the greatest husband in the world who is always there supporting everything I do with love, kindness and sacrifice helping me with whatever I need. Honey I can't thank you enough you are my hero. Thank you for fifteen wonderful years.

To my Mom who has stood by me through it all. I was privileged to have her as a source of support and prayer.

In memory of my Dad who always encouraged me to be and do anything I wanted to always follow my dreams and to my own self be true. Thanks Dad I miss you every day.

To all three of my sons and my daughter in laws who are always there to support and love me and their encouragement for me to follow my dreams has meant so much. Thank you for helping Mom make her dreams come true.

To my Grandchildren who I am so proud of and who provide the downtime I need to keep me sane. Thank you for being in my life you are each such a blessing.

Thank you to the men who have served our country who have been a source of information and inspiration to me. God Bless you all.

Thank you to the people in my life who inspired many of the characters in this book. Many from my past, those that have passed on and some from my present thank you all for your inspiration.

Thank you to my editors who try to make every line come out right.

A special thanks to Christian Kane who I had the distinct privilege of meeting in 2016. It was amazing to watch him work and have time to sit and talk with him. I hope one day, God willing, Project Solomon will be produced with Christian Kane as my director of choice.

ABOUT THE AUTHOR

L. W. Edwards enjoys a career in Medical Devices where she has been privileged to come in contact and work with some of America's finest servicemen.
Her curiosity of the paranormal has introduced her to those who enjoy the supernatural as much as she does.
She lives along the Minnesota River with her husband enjoying her gardens and as many books as her house can hold. To her there is no end to the adventure here or hereafter.

For more information visit www.blackonyxpress.com

SOLOMON INC. MYSTERIES

BONES OF MINE
(Solomon Inc. Mysteries, Book 1)

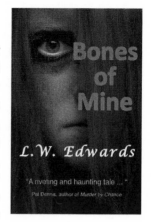

Addie Conroy, one of the senior partners in the international security firm Solomon Inc., only wanted to make sure that Lilly, the little girl who moved in next door, was safe. Having lived next to the little brick house for several years, Addie never expected that her investigation would open a door to the Other Side. Suddenly she discovered another little girl, who, as it turns out, has lived on the lane much longer than any of the current neighbors. They soon find that this little girl is the one who needs their help. Hired by Lilly's father to investigate the strange family curse that lead them from Canada to Minnesota, Addie and the firm are determined to help the spirits settle the unfinished business from another lifetime.

PIRATES ALLEY: The New Orleans Connection
(Solomon Inc. Mysteries, Book 2)

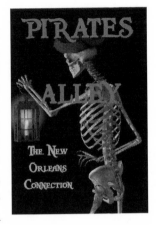

Investigator and junior Partner Addington Conroy of Solomon Inc. has the life she's always dreamed of, the perfect job, a house by the river and an incredible husband. But when questions surrounding the deaths of the companies two Founders lead her to believe they were murdered. Her instincts compel her back to New Orleans to investigate a case that Solomon Inc. hadn't closed. As she formulates a plan and chooses the team for her investigation, she's sidetracked by an interesting new client. It soon becomes apparent her client is yet another piece in a growing puzzle that will keep her in New Orleans longer than expected. It was New Orleans where she'd been called for an urgent meeting by her former partner Retired Admiral Isaac McClellan two years prior. Before the Admiral had a chance to tell her why he'd insisted they meet, he suffered an unexpected heart attack and died in her arms. Since the death of Admiral Isaac, new information had surfaced relating to the second of the two founders Retired Special Agent Secret Service Pavel Trask headquartered in Panama City. Addie and her team now suspecting the deaths of both men may have been murder, decide to split themselves between New Orleans and Panama. Following her lead, the teams are determined to find the truth behind the untimely deaths of their founders and the hidden secrets that surround Solomon Inc.

Made in the USA
Middletown, DE
20 May 2019